POLYGONIA

A Story of a Southern African Country

Henri Mervin

MINERVA PRESS
LONDON
MIAMI   RIO DE JANEIRO   DELHI

POLYGONIA: *A Story of a Southern African Country*
Copyright © Henri Mervin 2001

ISBN 0 75411 445 7

First Published 2001 by
MINERVA PRESS
315–317 Regent Street
London W1B 2HS

Printed in Great Britain for Minerva Press

POLYGONIA
A Story of a Southern African Country

Acknowledgements

I should like to tender my sincere and grateful thanks to Gerard Pitot, who so ably assisted me with both the computer and the installation and use of the printer, as well as to my good brother, Father Maurice, and my sons, Joseph and James, who lent a helping hand with the writing, the word processing and the printing.

About the Author

Henri Mervin was born in France in 1933 and studied in England at Downside School and the Royal London Medical College in Whitechapel, London. He qualified in 1958. He has worked in Africa for thirty-six years, twenty-eight of them in South Africa, usually in the casualty or surgical wards.

Joseph Khuzwayo

Joseph Khuzwayo was born in a village called Esigodeni, a name which means 'a place where gold had been found', though that was long ago. This small place – with a store, a garage, a school, a church and several brick houses together with a couple of hundred round mud-and-wattle walled huts with thick thatching dotted around the valley and along the hill sides – was typically rural. Its inhabitants had fields for their maize and cattle, and also kept pigs, chickens and a few donkeys. Joseph's father, Phineas, was one such farmer, using communal land for his four cattle plus the two acres for his maize crop which he could call his own.

Phineas had spent five years in one of the gold mines three hundred kilometres away, which had allowed him to buy his two acres from the tribal chief, the *induna*, as well as to pay for his wife. That was the custom there; the man paid for his wife, according to her value, the bride price or *lobola*, though it was true to mention that he had started his family long before this *lobola* had been completely paid off, and he soon had three girls and his son and heir, Joseph. After that, Phineas never left his land except once a year to buy grain seed and trinkets and clothes for his wife. All other transactions were done locally at the village or in the neighbourhood.

Five years after being settled so, he started suffering with a persistent cough which never quite went away. He tried the well-known *iboza* infusion treatment prescribed by the local witch doctor, or a *sangoma*, who, for a price of twenty rand, showed him how to use the leaves. (The South African rand is equivalent to one-tenth of an English pound, or one-sixth of a US dollar at this time.)

This infusion of leaves from a mint-like plant is taken at the rate of one tablespoon three times a day and is useful for treating many conditions like malaria, fevers, diarrhoea and general body pains. The concoction helped for a couple of weeks, but then the coughing resumed, together with sputum mixed with blood, known as haemoptysis. Before, when he'd had severe burns on the left side of his chest after falling against a red hot stove, he had treated this successfully with the leaves of the lily plant, *Bulbine latifola*, known locally as *ibucu*. The burns had healed in a week, in spite of a retired nurse's recommendation that he attend the local government hospital forty kilometres away for initial treatment, at least. So much for this Western style of medicine, he thought. However, once he began coughing up blood, he went to check in at the local Isibadlela Hospital. A chest X-ray showed he had bilateral pulmonary tuberculosis. For this, he was put on a six-month treatment of tablets to be collected each month at this rural clinic and hospital.

After three months of treatment, he was feeling so much better that he threw his TB tablets away and never went back to the hospital to finish the course, thinking to himself that the *abelungus*, or the whites, always exaggerated. For example, their houses were too big, their cars too big, their cities too big, and they themselves were often too big with swollen stomachs that made the men look as if they were eight months' pregnant.

Phineas thought that Dr John Watson, the white-haired old man at the hospital, with his insistence on six months of these filthy tablets, was merely providing another example of exaggeration. It was obvious that he was quite fit after three months of the horrid things, which tasted like horse manure and quite put him off his food.

One year after Phineas's prognostic assessment, he was back where he had been before, only slightly worse. So back again he went to the local clinic-hospital, and once again it was explained to him by that same Dr Watson that his condition had spread further than it had been over a year ago. He was kept in the TB ward for three months, while his maize crops and animals were being badly looked after by his wife and three children, the two younger girls and his only son, Joseph.

The eldest daughter had been married off by then, and her *lobola* had been mostly paid off except for one more cow and several hundred rand still promised and expected by the father, who knew from Zulu custom that the young man dared not fail him.

Again Phineas was discharged and told to follow another six months' treatment at home. But after another three months, making six in all plus the other three the year before, he felt so much better that he stopped the treatment again, only to find himself one year later with two scarred lungs and the tuberculous bacilli now resistant to nearly all effective treatment. He died of suffocation and inanition six months later. Dr Watson had warned him often of the serious nature of this condition. The doctor had used stern words of warning with careful descriptions of the awful consequences of defaulting, all to no effect.

Watson had seen too many examples of defaulters to be enthusiastic about cures until TB patients were shown to be completely and absolutely cured, as shown by negative sputum and negative culture for the pernicious TB bacilli. If Phineas had only kept to the original regime at the beginning, he would have been strong and fit to live another fifteen to twenty years easily, to the benefit of family, children and friends.

As it was, he was destined to die because of sheer carelessness combined with a complete misjudgement about the seriousness of his situation.

Joseph was ten by then and always remembered his father lying weakly in his own hut, near to but separate from his family's hut, as instructed, coughing bloodstained sputum and walking slowly with short panting breaths whenever he went outside to relieve himself among the wattle mimosa and erythrhynum trees. He also remembered his father's words, uttered with solemn intent, 'You, Joseph will have to lead the family soon, be strong and brave; don't waste your powers with drink, drugs and senseless fights. As you grow more, remember your father and your mother, who has been forever obedient to me. Always respect her. Be grateful for what you have, so as to increase your position with regards to other men, towards the spirits of the ancestors and to the great God of the universe. Do not let others get the better of you; keep to friends, not some strange acquaintance who might promise gain for yourself when in fact he calculates to rob or defame you. Goodbye, son and daughters, I will be watching from the mighty ancestral throne on the great mountains, the Drakensberg, known as *Izintaba Zokhahlamba* by the Zulu people.'

So Joseph always remembered these words of his father, whom he had esteemed for his discharge of duties to family and friends. He saw that his father's one big mistake had been not to follow the advice of professionals who obviously knew their trade. They were especially aware that two to three million people in the world die every year of pulmonary tuberculosis because they 'felt better'.

Joseph, Man of the Family

Joseph Khuzwayo became the only male and the man of the family at ten, with two older sisters; the eldest one had been married a year before and so was no longer part of the close family, though she still lived quite near by; and his middle-aged mother, Jabulile, who earned a living farming the cattle and maize and by sewing shirts for the better-off women of the area.

At the village of Esigodeni, Father Burley, a missionary priest, used to come twice a month to run a Christian service. He was a big man, six feet tall with a tidy beard and the typical brogue of someone coming from Cork. True to Irish tradition, he would speak Zulu badly during his sermons; but he would also avail himself of the services of an interpreter on occasions.

Joseph used to take an interest in these sermons because they were a form of instruction. His schooling had stopped at standard four when he was thirteen years old. He came to realise as he slowly grew to manhood that knowledge, understanding and learning were important influences. He understood tribal lore and the people's local history, together with the local farming knowledge, but there was so much more to know. There was the understanding of the machines that used to pass on the road near the village, the news of country and world affairs he might hear on the wireless, or the talk at the local store relating to more than just local gossip.

Later, men came to the village to talk to any and all the people who wanted to listen. These men, always no fewer than two, sometimes four, talked not so much of the past histories of the many tribes in the province, but of the future, and how the tribes must unite and act as one people and band together with a common purpose.

Father Burley usually ended his sermons with the phrase 'Nkulunkulu Nizonisiza' (God will help you people), but these visiting men were different. They would finish their talks with phrases like, 'We must arrange for ourselves,' or, 'We can provide for ourselves.'

It was a known fact that there were many groups in the area and beyond who spoke the same language, but that did not mean they were united as a common people with a common interest. Many kept memories of past wrongs and hurts concerning neighbouring people close by, or even not so close, but many kilometres away. These injustices of the past were not forgotten. In fact, they were remembered down through quite a few generations, so that a brave Zulu warrior might still easily creep up at dead of night with warrior friends to a set of huts where it was known that a clan lived whose grandfathers had killed off their grandfathers in serious quarrels about cattle ownership or *lobola* and wife injustices that had never been righted during the past sixty years. Their victims were not known personally to these young men, but their fate had been decided and so it was, 'Take this, you descendants of criminal dogs.' Thus, perhaps as many as six people might have been knifed and killed by the break of day when the other villagers stirred themselves for their usual early morning relief.

There were many such examples, never forgotten. It was the theme of these visiting men, Sipho and Nhlandla, that vendettas that were decades old should now be terminated everywhere in the burgeoning country of Polygonia. In a short time they were no longer considered as strangers and were listened to willingly. Young people found their talks encouraging because they wanted to believe in the Zulu unity which Sipho and Nhlandla talked about. Such young people found their talks meaningful and were keen to learn from them. Many elderly folk also came to hear the visitors and were pleased with this kind of talk.

Many used to say, 'If only you two (or you four, as the case may be) had come before, many lives now uselessly lost would have been saved. All because of some stupid revengeful thoughts about others we never even knew, the young ones were urged to kill, following the traditions of the elders. What the hell did it matter to us that grandfathers, or even great-grandfathers, had suffered death or disgrace? Quite likely, they themselves were guilty of some misdemeanour that we never heard about. Why the hell should our young people carry out a revenge on others quite unknown to us? If the original miscarriage of justice did in fact occur, it is a disaster that we should have to try to correct it. Those people back then should have done it, or else simply left it alone. It is not for us to try to redress a crime when it happened so long ago.'

This was how many would talk about these nonsensical vendettas. Many listening agreed with this kind of speech. They befriended the strangers, to tell them that with the permission of the ancestors, they wished to be absolved from the duties imposed with oaths and curses by their still living and unforgiving grandparents. They asked earnestly to be excused from the rites or needs of ancestral demands, and the strangers seemed able to absolve them by simply saying, 'This kind of revenge is no longer necessary or compulsory. We consider that you have more important duties to care about. So let it be!'

In this way, many felt freed from guilt or the shame of neglect and no longer feared the anger of avenging spirits who once were much to be feared and had dominated many generations.

But this change of heart and thoughts were not easy for the middle-aged and older people. The younger ones were not much bothered by the altered attitude, but for the others it disturbed their peace of mind. It involved a personal inner conflict which left many very troubled. Before, these ancient vendettas had been spoken of so often during their lifetime that this way of thinking had become something of a raison d'être or a reason for their very existence.

Whenever there were natural disasters, like massive floods that occurred every ten to fifteen years around January or February – the wet months of the year – or great hailstorms with big lumps of ice – some as big as billiard balls – that could destroy a year's harvest in twenty minutes, or large grass and forest fires which might happen twice in a lifetime – usually during the dry windy month of August – then the elder folk would turn to each other with grim faces and say solemnly, 'You see, the ancestors are angry and their spirits have sent a punishment upon us, because we did not appease their anger.'

This was the tradition embedded among these people of the

land who lived close to nature. This way of thinking was so etched in their way of judging or viewing their world that it was not easy for them to adopt another kind of philosophy.

Visitors

As time progressed, the village folk of Esigodeni were invited to more serious meetings. Mostly the young ones, the ones with the strength of youth and the vitality of enthusiasm, were encouraged to attend these gatherings, usually at a farmyard next to an open barn where many could gather without fear of interference. They were friendly and so interesting at the same time. That was when Joseph learned what living was all about. Before, he had had to be content with a routine of work with the maize, cattle, chickens and a few pigs. His only hope of getting a wife depended on his saving from the sale of his pigs to the local butcher and of his maize crops to the other farmers for their animals or to the local inhabitants for their needs. Saving money from such sales meant that it would take several years before he had enough for the bride price that all Zulu men must pay to get a wife. Joseph was not keen to spend five years working in the mines after seeing what had happened to his father.

Now, by listening to these visiting teachers, he came to see the importance of united action by his fellow men to achieve self-determination. The people around Esigodeni and elsewhere generally considered themselves as free people, but there were times when this was not really so. When roads were built near their village, strong roads with hard rocky surfaces, there was no one to object or prevent this hard road going straight over their land. If any of them managed to enter the big provincial cities, there were many places denied them, places where others ate and drank, places with big rooms and many chairs. Even on the beaches, there were areas for their own people and other places for the other peoples, the white man's areas and also the Asiatic areas where these Zulus were not welcomed. It did not bother them much, because they were not so keen to go to these places anyway. But it did show them that they were not masters nor accepted in many places of human activity.

Later when they were taxed on their profits, the men of Esigodeni and elsewhere were annoyed to be told that the finance went
towards making roads when they already had one, not as hard as
the new one but a road all the same; or they were told that the
finance was to pay soldiers and police for their protection, when
they were already quite well protected; or if there was a criminal
giving trouble, it annoyed them when neither the army nor the
police were there to stop such criminal interference. There was
the argument about finance going towards medical health
expenses, farming and education, but they still had to pay at least
one rand whenever they went to their Isibadlela clinic far away
and no farming development had ever been done in their area.
The schooling was always done by Mrs Mhlongo, to whom they
paid their one rand fee every month to help her run her class of
fifty children in the big barn next to the local church. Further,
those who listened to these government officials could not
imagine how any farming improvement could be done since all
their land was being used either for cattle grazing or under tillage
for their maize crops.

Further teachings by these visiting men, Sipho and Nhlandla,
became instructive rather than explanatory. There were explanations and instructions of the rights of men and women, with
claims that all had a right to work, earn and live by their labours,
according to the adage, 'From each according to his ability, to each
according to his needs.' From this was developed the idea of
justice that extended not only in the law courts, but to each and
every individual in regard to their rights and properties. There
was the explanation about the progress of mankind, seen in
history from the primitive Stone Age through to the present-day
capitalism of the moneyed people using the non-moneyed people
to their advantage. The socialist principle of each according to his
needs captivated the minds of Joseph Khuzwayo and his contem-
poraries, who felt that just such a socialist system was what they
could work at for their future good.

They discussed these ideas among themselves after the travelling teachers had gone, turning over in their minds how much
was true talk and how much was fancy or imagination. Mostly the
young people were keen and eager to go along with plans for a

united people, certainly among their Zulu-speaking tribes. To hell with all these revenge stories which the elders were so eager to implement and finalise for the sake of the ancestors' spirits that kept troubling them.

But they had to admit that unity and cooperation with Xhosas and Tswanas and many others might prove difficult. Even if a hand of friendship were extended to these many people, would they on their part agree to establish a working friendship when it was these people's ancestors who had suffered so much in the Zulu wars of the last century? The concept of unity was especially difficult when one considered how many different languages there were among these many different tribes. Would non-clicking blacks with different vocabularies and grammar be willing to work together with blacks using many clicks in the language that they loved when misunderstandings were so easy? It was considered worth trying; half-cooperation was better than complete non-cooperation.

Many of the inhabitants of Esigodeni were grateful to these visitors, Sipho and Nhlandla, for their instructive and descriptive lessons, which came to mean so much to those who listened. They were asked to come again, to bring along some of their other friends, and to feel free to visit as friends and brothers of the Zulu confraternity. In fact, the people of Esigodeni were glad to have visitors at their village when so few people normally came to visit, and especially was this true when these men and their friends were so engaging in their conversation.

The young people were really keen to talk more with the travelling teachers. Their talk was much more meaningful than the usual talk in the area, when the young people were told persistently to care for the cattle and keep the herds safe. It was the duty of the young boys to look after the herds of their fathers and grandfathers all day as well as at night, to see that the beasts were protected against thieves or predators, like the occasional lion looking for an easy meal. These teachers talked with a kind of knowledge which was not forced upon them, but extended a kind of invitation.

Abroad

Several months after their first lessons in the village of Esigodeni, the young people were invited to commit themselves to further serious training at a place far away. Those interested were to bring an identity book and one hundred rand in cash. Joseph's mother did not understand what this training was about, even after questioning Joseph, and presumed it was a training similar to that of other young men who had left before to follow Fr Burley's example, and who had returned later as very clever preachers.

Joseph Khuzwayo left in a crowd of fifty-four, ten of them women. They travelled by car, bus, a train he'd never seen before, and then they walked into Mozambique. From thence, more buses, another train, and finally a large camp south of Dar-es-Salaam. Their quarters were two huts of earthen walls and corrugated iron roofs with a third smaller hut for the women. Discipline was draconian. Up at day break; a ten kilometre jog; a breakfast of porridge with salt; trench digging, arms drill; lessons on patrolling, hand grenades, landmines and, most important, the assembling and dismantling of the light machine gun. Then instructions on hygiene, wound care, understanding of disease, that is, parasites as in malaria, bacteria of all kinds and finally viruses. Then there were classes about diet, eating for health and a short course on cooking methods; all most instructive. Above all, there were the lessons teaching political science according to Marxist–Leninist theories, though none of them actually heard these names mentioned.

When Joseph had left Esigodeni, his only language was Zulu, a language of Southern Africa and probably five thousand years old, considering its complexity. After six weeks at Camp Kosi, he was speaking usable English, plus Swahili phrases learned at the local store, one kilometre from the camp, to which they were allowed twice weekly. Swahili he found quite easy to learn; many words were similar to his own and it had none of the peculiar clicking sounds that his own language had, like someone trying to suck food debris out from a tooth cavity.

Joseph and his peers were grateful for the chance to learn. His last lessons at Esigodeni had been reading stories like 'The Porcupine Goes to Earth' and 'Why the Chameleon Squints'.

The teachers at Camp Kosi taught him the meaning of life and of the universe. He learned about the progress of mankind from the early communities of the Stone Age through to feudalism, capitalism and the final socialistic society, the society of from each according to his ability and to each according to his needs, where there is no central government, no capitalist system, and the chance of the possession of the means of production by the proletariat, which meant the workers of the world like himself. There would be a centrally planned economy with the revolutionaries so transforming human nature as to render the state superfluous, except for innocuous functions like deciding where roads might be built and which persons deserved further education.

Their political philosophy was a natural creed, with no belief in the supernatural world. They were taught that religion is the opium of the people, a spiritual drug through which the capitalistic slaves forget their human rights and their just demands for a life worthy of man. Joseph wondered how Fr Burley would respond to all these different kinds of teachings. He went along with it because it was a sort of education and, further, it would be unwise to disagree with teachers who might easily take exception and become angry with anyone daring to disagree.

The first eight weeks were the most interesting. After that the lessons were more complicated and not easily learned. Some of the young men wanted more freedom to travel to the big city of Dar-es-Salaam and more money for their visits. Free periods were increased, but allowances weren't, since there was no more finance for the fifty-four young people. This was easily solved by some of the young blades. While two of them distracted the attention of a shop cashier, a third would empty the till of money and walk away slowly if unnoticed, or slip away fast if anyone had seen him. It was a practice they had used in the big towns in South Africa and many were the times they could walk away quite calmly with two minutes to spare before anything was found missing. Eventually, some were caught after several such escapades and their identity uncovered and disclosed at Camp Kosi. The punishment was severe; eighteen lashes with a bamboo cane, two weeks' solitary with bread and water, then two months with no leave and double night duties with sentry postings, plus daily sewage cleaning. This stopped the stealing for several months and the civic authorities were assured that the culprits had been suitably punished and corrected. When robberies did start again, many months later, there were very few incidents and the guilty ones were never caught. While the first batch had learned not to steal, the few robberies that did occur much later were done by robbers who had learned not to be caught.

Six months into training, the vanguard socialist progressives from Esigodeni were taught how to be instructors. They were shown how to pick men capable of learning and leading. They were taught to use their words persuasively so as to teach the inevitable progress of scientific socialism. They came to understand that their world was a complex of matter, finance and psychology. They were told there was no God; the universe had laws of its own with no higher creator.

Joseph Khuzwayo wondered how God would feel when people ceased to believe in him. He came to know about the big bang theory in astronomy, organic evolution of the animals and plants, and the influence of the subconscious mind, working with or against the conscious mind. Above all, he learned that, 'When you're in charge, it's your world that works. When a reactionary capitalist is in charge, you work to undermine his status.'

Camp Kosi

Eight months into training, it was found that one of the young women was four months pregnant. She was pressured to have an abortion or a termination of pregnancy, but she resisted. She was told that foetuses were a hindrance to socialist progress.

She replied that it was part of progress to nurture the future with care and love for the next generation. She was told that love was a sensation-hormonal feeling only compatible with bourgeois romantic affections. She insisted that a foetus of socialist parents and in a similar environment would surely be endowed with innate tendencies towards socialist revolution and reform. She insisted on keeping what she considered was part of herself, and by virtue of her agile, wilful reasoning, she was allowed to carry to term provided she would be able to care for the child at Camp Kosi or anywhere else, and that she revealed who the father was. She insisted on her ability to look after the child because of her own health, her family experiences and the camaraderie around her which gave her much reassurance. But she refused to reveal who her escort was, since it was only her concern. They, the disciplinary authorities, could consider any one of the forty-four Zulu men as the father, it did not matter. Nobody knew who the father was except Nonhlanhla and Joseph Khuzwayo. He was very proud of her insistence on a full-term pregnancy and delivery, and of her persistent and insistent silence about his fatherhood.

But he lived in an agony of suspense, separated from her most of the time when he wanted to share time with and to help her, to hold her and say how much she meant to him. To reassure her, he said how they would soon return to the province of Natal and work and share a life together so as to make a worthy future for themselves and everyone around.

'Courage,' he used to say, 'Bekezela, and we will be strong together. Just have faith in me.'

The disciplinary committee were concerned about the implications of this fertility and applied for advice to the headquarters for moral supervision of Marxist theory in Dar-es-Salaam with regard to any action that should be taken. They were told quite clearly that this was a matter for the camp leaders to decide on. Their own decisions were concerned with murder, drug dealing, international crime and socialist ideologies to be taught in schools and universities. This left the camp leaders free to decide and to act on their own without any fear of blame or misjudgement; what a relief, instead of being told what to do.

The last phase of teaching was called 'Revolution and Explosion'. It meant the understanding and the use of force for the cause of progress. Old systems cannot be adapted to new ways. It is necessary to have explosions to do away with old hardened systems, and then the new system will supersede and become the way of the future. Capitalism was constantly exposed as a system of greedy selfish colonialists who had imposed their will on many countries, Polygonia included. Polygonia was the name these teachers had given to the eastern lands of South Africa, from where all the students of Kosi Camp originated. This land had developed typically as a result of the arrangements of adventurers who had turned to a labour system of profit through their knowledge of farming and in industry. These men were the sons and grandsons of those who had left the old countries of Europe and had managed to establish themselves through their techniques in a country originally peopled mostly by nomadic black African tribes. Two centuries later their descendants were in command of all the productive functions that any large country contains: farming, mining, trading, manufacturing and all the services like education, the health services, roads and communications. So the young men and women at Kosi Camp learned the need for these national, provincial and even parochial firms, companies and industries to be always in the possession of the white immigrants, adventurers and settlers. This had come to be accepted as the natural development in any country, especially as in Africa!

The young people of Kosi Camp learned that such arrangements were not meant to last. They, the youth and flower of their tribes and of the people, were the future masters of their land with all that it contained. It was by education and technology that they were to become masters, which before had been left to the elitist white bosses. Education was emphasised as necessary for all serious progress, that is, knowledge of technology, engineering, chemistry, physics and so on, as well as the ability for clear expression. The importance of language was stressed. They were made to realise that correct statements with extensive explanations or concise details were far superior to slick phrases, worn clichés and ugly swear words that often caused a reduction of understanding and an increase in resentment.

After two years of this Spartan-style training, the group to which Joseph Khuzwayo belonged were ready for repatriation and for exercising leadership work in and among their own people. They no longer numbered fifty-four. Two young men had died of stab wounds from the petty fighting that so easily breaks out amongst hot-headed young men. Three had died of malaria in spite of the precautions; the clearing and drainage of marsh lands all around the camp, the use of prophylactic medicines and the use of mosquito nets at night. Guard duties at night around the camp, when the men were most vulnerable to mosquito attacks, were the cause of this sickness.

Of the three convicted and punished for serious theft, two had escaped, never to be heard of again in the camp called Kosi. They were in fact killed by bandits east of Mpanda in Tanzania, after stealing sheep and hiding in the forests of the Uppi Highlands. Bandits were habitually in hiding there and they resented the intrusion of strangers.

Although seven had died, never to see again their homelands again, one was added to their number. Nonhlanhla had a fine son. The birth was normal, assisted by two women accustomed to help in these natural functions. The son was cared for by the ten women present, each taking turns to change nappies, to wash him and to console him when the child was fretful, but naturally the main carer for the child was its mother. Nonhlanhla breastfed him and played with him in between kitchen duties, arms drill, gun technology training and the frequent talks on scientific socialism, about the progress to the future. This future, to be nurtured by the present, would eventually embody a classless society for such people as her son, Nimrod, the name of the mighty hero of Babylon and Assyrian towns long ago. His name connoted both a great builder of towns and kingdoms as well as a rebel from the Hebrew tradition, symbolic of defiance against the God of the Old Testament. Perhaps, Nonhlanhla thought, her Nimrod, now eighteen months old, would likewise build up his own people and act in defiance of the superstitions of the Western capitalistic system. People of her background believed in very different values which he might bring to the fore again. This Nimrod might live to show the irrelevance of God as taught to Nonhlanhla by her previous teachers. He was now considered dead and gone, merely a source of mythological stories that the new age could dispense with advantageously.

This was the position when this brave band of student warriors left Kosi Camp early to go by bus, train, bus again, then a sixty-kilometre trek – easy after all their training – past the arid wastelands south of Komatipoort, where they avoided policemen and other officers, to meet finally south of the Kruger Park with their new leaders. Then they headed into the pregnantly expectant land of Natal, a province of Polygonia.

Early Beginnings

The country right at the southern tip of the African continent goes by the name of South Africa from its geographical position, though it might just as well be called Polyglossia, a place of many tongues. It is a great mixture of different peoples. It was a land not farmed for centuries, with only occasional roving bands of Hottentots and Bushmen. Then Zulus, Shangaans, Xhosas and Sothos arrived and wandered too, living nomadic lives among the hills, mountains, plains and valleys. The only records they have left are graves, simple buildings and stone fortifications which are now at ground level; the rest has been removed by time or other men's devastation, which was just as complete.

In the seventeenth century, a substantial change came with the arrival of Europeans. There were the Portuguese who rounded the Cape of this vast continent in 1498 and later left two colonies on both sides, later called West and East Portuguese Africa; much later, with the wave of decolonisation they were called Angola and Mozambique. Then Hollanders came and settled in the Cape area where they established a viable shipping station, harbour, settlement, and then a settlers' colony that grew and spread. It didn't stop spreading for many years. It expanded from the confines of that small settlers' area, and three centuries later had come to cover one and a half million square miles or two million square kilometres, if you want it in the metric measurements. But the growth and spread of these early Hollanders was not as simple as any organic growth. It went ahead with considerable strife and difficulties, as does any human endeavour.

The student of history will be interested to read accounts and reports made about this land. The manuscript accounts are now held in museums and archives for safe-keeping and they give an interesting story of increasing acquaintance with the area made by many Europeans and Asiatics who sailed by the southern part of the great African continent.

There is the report made by Herodotus, the Father of History, in the fifth century BC, which describes a journey of three years' duration carried out by Phoenician ships round the continent from their country to the Red Sea and back again.

> 'These men made a statement which I do not believe,' writes Herodotus, 'though others may, to the effect that as they sailed on a westerly course round the southern end of Libya, they had the sun on their right, and to the north of them. This is how Libya was first discovered to be surrounded by sea...' (Book Four, p.42, *The Histories*)

After this early recording there came many others much later on from the fifteenth century onwards. The first of these of significance is by Bartholomeu Diaz in 1488, who sailed with two ships down the coast of Africa. The crew became wearied and were greatly afraid of the heavy seas through which they had passed, but the captain, Diaz, persisted for a few more days around the coast. He wished to call the Cape area, 'Tormentoso', but King João, it is said, when told of the journey back in Portugal, gave it a more illustrious name, calling it, 'The Cape of Good Hope', because it promised the discovery of India via the southern route so longed for and sought after for so many years.

In 1497, Vasco da Gama went as commander of four ships on a voyage of discovery in search of spices. At the Cape, his crew bartered three bracelets for a black ox. They dined off it on a Sunday; it was very fat and the flesh was as savoury as those in Portugal. They continued beyond the journey of Diaz and 'it pleased God that we should make good journey to Mozambique and from there to return and reach their country in August 1499'.

In 1595, a century later, Cornelius de Hortman relates more about the people of Africa, and trade really got going; a fine ox for a poor cutlass and a copper adze; two more oxen for a new copper adze; then three oxen and three sheep for a seventy-pound iron rod and three oxen and five sheep for an old knife, a shovel, an iron bolt with another knife and iron scraps. The natives are described as of small stature, red brown, and entirely naked but for an ox hide around them like a cloak with a wide thong of leather around their waists, of which one end hung before their privies. Some had wooden boards under their feet instead of shoes. They always stank greatly since they besmeared themselves with fat and grease. They made fires very quickly by twisting one piece of wood against another; thus they passed the nights and such fires one saw every night in various places. When any oxen were killed by the sailors, they begged for the entrails, which they ate raw after shaking out most of the dung, or stretched it over the fire on four sticks for a short time, then ate it. 'We could learn no more of them but that they speak very clumsily like the folk in Germany who suffer from goitre.' Another from the same crew described their speech as being just as if one heard a number of angry turkeys, little else but clucking and whistling.

Sir James Lancaster, in 1601, with three ships, describes a stay in the area, again trading with metal pieces for ox and sheep:

> and the people of this place are all of a tawnie colour, of a reasonable stature, swift of foot and much given to picke and steale; their speech is wholey uttered through their throat and they click with their tongues in such sort that in seven weeks we remained heere in this place, the sharpest wit amongst us could not learne one word of their language, yet the people would soon understand any signe we made to them.

The crew were evidently glad to stay here, for Sir James describes how,

> We had so royale a refreshing that all our men recovered their health and strength, only foure or five excepted, but before our coming in we had lost out of all our ships one hundred and five men.

Edward Terry writes in 1616 to say,

> these people, of all metals seem to love brass best, with which they make rings to wear on their wrist. These savages had their cattle which we bought off them at a very good command, for with a call, they would presently run to them; and when they had sold any one of their bullocks to us, they would by the same call make the poor creatures break from us and run to them again and by this trick now and then sell the same beast unto us two or

three times.

Edward Terry continues to describe how three years before,

On one of the company's ships, when she was ready to sail for England and having two of these savages aboard, the commander resolved to bring them both home with him, thinking that when they had some English here, they might discover something of their country which we could not know before. These poor wretches being brought away, very much against both their minds, one of them died shortly after they put to sea; the other who called himself Cooree lived and was brought to London, and kept there for the space of six months, in Sir Thomas South's house, then governor of the East India Company, where he had good diet, good lodging; he had made for him of bright brass an armour, breast and back and head piece with buckler all of brass, his beloved metal. Yet all this contented him not. When he had learnt a little of our language, he would daily lie upon the ground, and cry very often thus in broken English, 'Cooree home go, Souldania go, home go.' And when he had returned in 1614, he had no sooner set footing on his own shore but presently he threw away his cloaths, his linen with all covering and got his sheep skin back upon his back.

After this fellow was returned, it made the natives most shy of us when we arrived there, for they would come thither in great companies whenever we were newly come thither, yet three or four days before they conceived we would depart thence, there was not one of them, fearing alike we would have dealt with some of them as formerly we had done with Cooree. But it had been well if he had not seen England; for certainly when he came home he told his countrymen that brass was but a base and cheap commodity in England; then we had never after such a free exchange of our brass and iron for their cattle. It was here that I asked Cooree, 'Who was their God?' He lifting up his hands answered, 'England God, great God, Souldania no God.'

In 1622, Augustin de Beaulieu, with ships from Harfleur, describes how he was unable to discover in them any religion, but nevertheless they marry and dance and what is marvellous and yet true is that they have a testicle removed at the age of ten or twelve years or earlier. He was not able to know for what superstition or reason 'unless it be to run better and in truth they surpass all others that I have ever seen, and I believe that it would be hard to catch unless we were all mounted'.

Thomas Herbert, in 1627, describes the natives being privileged with charm both in visage and in nature:

> By way of dress, some shave their skull; some half the head; others leave a tuft on top; others have dresses for their head, brass buttons, pieces of pewter, beads of any sorts which the mirthful sailor exchanges for mutton, beef, herbs, ostrich eggs, tortoises and the like. Some we saw were semi-eunuchs and some women use excision, through custom or imitation rather than religion. It is reported that women are delivered without help or pain, and here the women give suck, the uberous dugg being stretched over their shoulder!
>
> And though these be treacherous yet doubtless they esteem more an Englishman than a Portuguese or a Fleming by the friendship and good dealing our men use of them.

The Country

But all these events happened a long time ago, and the seventeenth century ships' logs reveal as much about their writers' views as about those they met. The present-day situation is very different. It is no longer a question of foreign ships calling on the coast of Polygonia to resupply with cattle, fruit and fresh water; it's a question of who owns what, where and how.

The Dutch at the southern tip of the country expanded as farmers, while the Portuguese settled in the east and west first as traders and then as farmers. Later, the British arrived. Their purpose was to stem the French corsairs and pirates who were causing so much trouble during the Napoleonic Wars, and once they were established from around 1801 onwards, they stayed, and spread. The Dutch were by now changed and called Afrikaners, and as they spread, they came to dislike their own people's authority at Cape Town as well as that of the British, with whom they couldn't speak easily since their languages were so different. Later, they even began fighting each other over rights of nationality and property rights, which meant they were fighting about who was in authority. Both sides thought they were in charge with their own powers of command. After the fighting, called the Boer Wars, it was the British who were in control, for the time being anyway. That was in 1901, just after Queen Victoria's death. By this time, the country was spread over two million square kilometres; a land with the usual mountains, rivers, valleys and deserts, such as can be found in any large land masses.

But it must be understood that this large land mass was not only occupied by European settlers; there lived there also millions of native Africans, that is, black men and women, distinguished by their dark skin, short tightly curled hair, thick lips and broad noses. These peoples had occupied the land for thousands of years, perhaps ten to twenty thousand years. They were known as Zulus, Sothos, Tswanas, Shangaans, Xhosas and other smaller groups, the Ndebeles, Tongas and Vendas. These people have survived through the centuries by hunting, and with a partial pastoral economy; they had learned how to grow the maize plant, after the Portuguese had shown them the advantages of this cereal; and sorghum grown long before maize; they also herded cattle. Cattle constituted their wealth; they were kept herded together as they moved around in different land areas, and increased at a low compound interest rate. There had been many examples of cattle stealing and intertribal conflict, so that inevitably these different tribes were not united, far from it. Different groups maintained their sense of supremacy with their stories of the historical achievements of the ancestors. Further, their different languages separated them seriously in that each man and woman were known instantly by their speech; and when some did not belong in an area, they were evicted with family and belongings, or worse still, simply annihilated.

These events can be read in any modern history book where small groups are described frequently at loggerheads with each other. Nowadays, this has changed from small to large groups being at loggerheads. Pleas for unity were often repeated by valiant leaders, and over the years their pleas had an effect; hence the small groups of united peoples became large groups of partially united peoples. Anyone who travels around in the large country of Polygonia would be struck by the great differences among the various people. There are the town dwellers living in townships outside big cities or towns, who travel daily to the towns for their work and their salaries. These townships can accommodate over a million people, as does the town of Soweto outside the metropolis of Johannesburg. Cape Town has Khayelitsha, Gugulethu and Mitchell's Plain area with one million coloureds, the legacy of Dutch and other traders' fertility. Durban has many townships also: Umlazi, Kwamashu, Isibingo and others. Out in the countryside, rural life, you see, is really different from the previous places mentioned. There are many mud-walled huts, thatched and usually rounded, together with cattle pens called kraals. These people do not have a salaried income, but live off their cattle, chickens, and maize crops, perhaps supplemented with the income of one of their men working far away. Those people with their huts and kraals in the distant hills and valleys will have received little schooling, if any. The elder folk of these areas find it impossible to know their ages, for example, and will consider moving forty kilometres as wandering into an unknown and a strange land. This is a common situation throughout the country. Many have lived so long in one small area that anywhere else is considered foreign country and best avoided.

It could be said that better education would help to correct these xenophobic attitudes, which is doubtless true, but any such programme of development takes time and needs an infrastructure of schools which cannot be established overnight. In fact, it has been estimated that worthwhile education takes two generations to produce a significant change for the better. Missionaries have tried over several centuries to effect valuable teaching in many different areas, often well supported with foreign finance. These fine examples of betterment were, however, too widespread; many places were not touched at all by these evangelical enthusiasts. Furthermore, the bible teachers were mostly concerned with teaching writing and reading to enable the students to read the Scriptures, and be able to read and teach others of the community who were prepared to learn, and so not have to depend on foreign teachers all the time.

There were certain government bodies in the early twentieth century who considered that all teaching up to standard five, that is, up to the average age of twelve, should be nationalised. Praiseworthy as all these missions had been in teaching and training, it was estimated that a national programme to cover the whole country, giving each and every person a chance of some kind of education, however elementary it might be to start with, must be implemented as soon as finance and materials allowed.

That is how hopeful organisers thought. That is, those men who had a real interest in the country's people, and were not just calculating for financial gain or pleasure. They used to say that education was everybody's right, not just a privilege.

The Descendants

It is now suitable and instructive to consider the history of the early settlers and colonists in the country of South Africa. The first arrivals were Dutchmen who came to the Cape area to stay as permanent residents.

The descendants of the original Dutch settlers are now known as Afrikaners. They have their own language, changed from the old Dutch language, but still recognisably Dutch. Their history dates from the settlement of Van Riebeeck, who started a colony at Cape Town in AD 1653. His descendants and those of his fellow settlers are now spread throughout South Africa, even extending farther into neighbouring countries like Zimbabwe, Namibia, Botswana, Swaziland, and even Mozambique and Angola. They are a sturdy, resolute people.

They are proud of their history and consider that the development of their country is largely due to the efforts of their predecessors. These people number around three million and, with three centuries of history to their credit, they rightfully consider their country as their own property. Of course, they have their divisions. Some believe in total control and consider that they have a God-given mission of authority and direction. Others are more accommodating in their dealings with the non-Afrikaner population. They concur with the need for full cooperation with the other settlers of non-Dutch origin. That means mostly those of British origins, who likewise are spread throughout each and every town and city. Then there are Germans, Greeks, Italians and Portuguese, to name the other main groups. Furthermore, these people, with their more relaxed attitude, believe in the necessity of cooperation with the original native black peoples. They believe in a confederacy of administration where people of many backgrounds are to work together in a system for multi-group planning and progress. They trust in the work ability of multiracial sharing. It is the differences between the Afrikaner

33

people that make for angry disagreements and give rise to outbursts of fury and even manslaughter.

Those who insist on total control consider their authority superior and more trustworthy than that of other peoples, whoever they may be. Their authority has been developed over three centuries of farming, land development, and concomitant town and city constructions and commerce. They have become accustomed to the difficulties of their country in their various guises, and, now confronted with the demands of a democracy that many millions proclaim as their right, they insist that any democracy is a pure fantasy at this stage of many people's development. They say that democracy demands responsibility, ability and respect, and it is just these qualities that are absent. The compliant cooperative types of Afrikaner consider cooperation as an important development which must be allowed to avoid the faults of autocracy and tyranny which can so easily develop otherwise. These latter consider that some cooperation is a form of progress that must be permitted even if there are violent disturbances.

The total control types consider that this is the whole point demanding proper understanding. Where there might be difficulties of a violent sort, there should be strict direction and discipline. In the years preceding this time, there was a policy developed by the National Party of the country called 'apartheid'. Some people thought this word meant 'hating apart'. But this is not the meaning of the word. The real meaning of the word is 'separate development'. This meant that white or European and pseudo-European populations had their own schools, hospitals, living areas and even buses and park benches, toilets and beach areas. The other peoples of the country, that is the black, semi-black, coloureds and Asiatics had their own hospitals, schools, living areas, buses, toilets and beach areas. There were several thousand painful resettlements, but the underlying trouble was not that some sections of the population were restricted in their movements and in their place of habitation. As far back as 1952, many different leading Christian churchmen began to denounce the fundamental injustice of the situation. The party in power had taken on itself the right of determining the status, rights and the political activity of the rest of the population.

In addition there was the strict Immorality Act, whereby it was illegal for a white-European type to have intimate sexual contact with one across the colour bar. Normally the question of adultery and fornication is left to the conscience of persons in accordance with what he and she considers suitable or correct. But in this example, the laws of South Africa had become statutory laws, whereby it was illegal for anyone to transgress the colour line. Any who did was guilty of a serious felony. It was a cruel law for those whites who loved blacks, or coloureds who loved whites, or blacks who loved coloureds and whites. But it did have certain good results. There were those descendants of Dutchmen who were so lusty and lascivious that they would fondle, cuddle and even copulate with anything that caught their fancy, caring not a tittle or a jot for the consequences of miscegenation, and this law did constrain their actions to a large extent. Many coloureds had been fathered by travelling Dutchmen on a willing black escort hoping for a week of meals. The resulting offspring never knew their fathers and came to disdain their mothers. Such people, so often abandoned, came to form a large group in the Cape area and now number over one million, resourceful and capable in their large communities; but still somehow many often still carry with them the mark of having been abandoned.

That did not condemn them as nasty nor horrible people. Not at all. These large groups of coloureds were often the most charming and loveable people, and once one had their trust and respect, they were really worth knowing and having as a reliable and trustworthy friends. Likewise, it can be stated that some of them could be really cunning and dangerous criminals. It is simply a question of not making generalisations but checking each on his own merits.

SADOFAC

Johannes Venter was the leader of 'Sons and Daughters of Farmers and Commerce', a group of realistic resourceful Afrikaners, known by the acronym SADOFAC. These young and enthusiastic people were the direct descendants of settlers in South Africa, anything like four to twelve generations after their ancestors had arrived and stayed in this large country. Their people had spread over two million square kilometres of land, were united by their language, their common biblical Christian creed and their love of this country with its very varied geography. Their land was bordered on three sides by the Atlantic and Indian Oceans and in the north by a great big central African river which flowed for three-quarters of the year and for the rest of the year was a series of deep pools and sandbanks. That's how many of the rivers are in this continent. Low wetlands, rocky coastlines, deserts, mountains, valleys, high plateaux were scattered with cities, towns, dorps or just hamlets.

A person was either a member of the Afrikaans clan by birth or he was an *uitlander*. No one could pretend to be an Afrikaner if he was not one. Johannes Venter had under his influence about ten thousand men and women, who were ready to stand to and act as guardians for their fatherland, and with that number there were another fifty thousand, wives and younger sons and daughters together with elderly men, ready to stand by these people even though they were not full members of SADOFAC. The full members had gone through simple rifle and platoon training, as well as basic military tactics; but most important had been the establishment of allegiance and unity among all these ten thousand members. Their policy was that of keeping their property and helping others to keep theirs, in accordance with the Dutch motto 'Je maintiendrai'. They were like a private civilian defence force.

At the same time, South Africa had its own regular national

defence force of about one hundred thousand soldiers, the SADF, plus the usual police force for civil use. It might be thought that South Africa was at this stage in a martial state, ready for war, but this is only because these military figures have been mentioned. There were millions of people with their farming, trading, mining and white-collar jobs with no thought of military conflict. As it happened, they were all to be involved later, in one way or another.

Johannes Venter was confident that his men were ready for conflict at six hours' notice. Their main concern was property protection for their own kind. This was possible in cities and towns where half the people were on their side without actually being armed. They could deploy platoons, disguised or in paramilitary clothes, where there were troubles like mob violence or demonstration marches that turned into violence with looting and general hooligan behaviour.

Such protection on farms was much more difficult and the farmers and families were indeed quite vulnerable. Already at this time elderly couples and isolated people were being killed in their homes, their belonging taken, usually in the owner's car or truck. These acts were mostly by blacks of the criminal class who lived by murder and robbery. Some quarter of this group would be caught later and imprisoned for several years by the police. The rest, not caught, changed their names, lodgings, village or continued pretending to be someone else.

Venter and his people were well aware of these events, as were the police. They encouraged these farmers at risk and isolated to be always alert and suspicious of unknown groups on their lands. But many farmers remained very vulnerable. Groups intent on robbery and crime could always hide during the day; strike in the early evening on the lonely isolated places; kill if they were obstructed, otherwise tie up the victims and gag them; take wirelesses, television sets, clothes, money, jewellery; pile it all into a truck or car nearby, all in fifteen minutes; and be off to the black African townships perhaps twenty or thirty kilometres away. By the time the robberies and break-ins had been discovered by neighbours and guards, it was usually twelve hours or more after the event.

The SADOFAC recorded these events and crimes of all kinds in all the detail possible. Over a couple of years it became apparent that those breaking in were interested in more than just finance. Increasingly valuable property was left behind in favour of arms, rifles, ammunition, anything that had military value. This alerted the SADOFAC members and made them conscious of the possible armed conflict that certain political groups often used to talk about.

What the members gained on the swings, they lost on the roundabouts, to use a well-worn English phrase. As these people improved their vigilance and security in the towns and cities, they also realised that they were losing their security and influence in the farmlands. Whilst they encouraged the use of telephone and short-range wireless among the remote crofters and farmers, they saw that they could never anticipate nor protect the widespread farming community. It was understood that lonely people must either defend themselves or simply become victims.

It had been the same story twenty years before in Rhodesia, now called Zimbabwe, and before that in other countries like Kenya. For fourteen years, Mr Ian Smith had led his Rhodesian Front, with the white settlers in command, while the growing African population were considered secondary citizens. For fourteen years there had been increasing military actions involving the Rhodesian army, police and their voluntary civilian force, but African military development and actions had never been stopped. Eventually, the latter became the rulers; the settlers became co-inhabitants, but no longer the rulers. There had been the same sequence of events, of murders on farmlands, then in towns with bombs, ambushes, typical guerrilla warfare. The SADOFAC were aware of the similarities and they did not wish events to take this path towards African autocracy. Of course, their country was different; there were many more settlers in South Africa than in Zimbabwe, and they had been in their country for three centuries compared to less than one century in Zimbabwe. Furthermore, the white Zimbabwean settlers had usually had a foot in another country. They were able, in many cases, to return to England or find a place in South Africa, or start again in Canada and Australia. The white settlers in South Africa were now indigenous Africans and had nowhere else to go. This country was their country and they intended to remain there and to be in command of the country which they considered their own. They had no wish to travel off to faraway places, into unknown lands, and to be among strange peoples with whom it would be difficult to make friends, even if these strangers did want to be friends! The chances were that foreigners abroad would be inimical for years ahead. It takes years to make friends, and after the age of forty, friends are even more difficult to establish. And that is only part of the problem. Who can simply start a career all over again in a faraway place from scratch, just because there were some shootings and killings? How many acquaintances of South African citizens had left, hoping to settle in greener pastures, only to come back two or four years later with stories of misfortune and loss of income, lack of friends, and what is more, the same violence elsewhere as in their old country, in their beloved town, farm or workplaces? Many expatriates were glad to be back, even with a loss of status, income or, most certainly, the loss of their old property. That is how the old settler citizens saw the situation, and with good reason. It was for this that the eager young people of SADOFAC were so keen to maintain their strength and command. Who can blame them?

There had been a group of Dutch-Afrikaners who had left the country after the last Boer War to settle in Argentina. Eighty years later, they were still there with their cattle farming, their language and their religion, a Calvinist group with strongly based biblical beliefs. Is this what emigrants were expected to experience? Perhaps it was, but the residents of South Africa were more interested in remaining in their old country and trying to survive any difficulties.

Club Talk

Johannes Venter was pleased with the progress of his men, spread out and devoted to the cause in the four provinces of South Africa. He believed the black African peoples, and there were seven large tribes of them in the land, wanted to take over his country and rule it as they had done in Zimbabwe, Mozambique, Angola, Zaire and many other countries whose mention is hardly necessary at this stage. He and his followers had no wish at all that their country should go the way of these other countries. If they were not to be in control of their country with its four provinces, at least they intended to be capable of directing its progress and its development. There had been many examples of men and women who had joined up with SADOFAC, for the sake of the training and the meetings of its members. They believed in the value of their own group with its leadership qualities. The fact that many large cities of South Africa are comparable to large cities through-out the world was testimony to the effectiveness of their own people's abilities over many years. Likewise, the farmers of that group were the backbone of the country's food production. They boasted of being able to produce forty to sixty bags of maize per acre of land with correct methods of ploughing, fertilising, weed control and sometimes overhead irrigation; they were not like the 'soil scratchers', with their over-grazing and the dreadful soil erosion that usually followed, who habitually produced five to seven bags of maize per acre and whose cattle would produce a calf only every three to ten years, with which they were quite satisfied, instead of annual calving.

Many young people had taken an interest in training and meeting with fellow compatriots, each with their own interests, but finally their heart was not fully in the organisation, so that they stayed as loyal members without being fully involved. It was a familiar pattern: safe living produces no energetic urgent involvement in self-defence.

But it must not be thought that Johannes Venter's men were all common burgers and peasant stock from seventeenth-century Holland. Many of these stalwart leaders were educated men with university degrees, with professional posts in medicine, law and finance; to think of the Afrikaner as just a peasant backbone of the country is a grave misjudgement.

Furthermore, the country had been greatly improved by immigrants during the later part of the seventeenth century when Protestants came from France where they were being persecuted. That was the age of religious intolerance. Nowadays, this intolerance is forgotten, taken over by less important matters like differences in political affiliations or whether a person is wealthy or poor. Cardinal Richelieu and, later, King Louis XIV, known to some historians as Louis Carthorse, hoped for a religiously united country; something very difficult and, in fact, impossible to obtain in a country like France. When it was found that various cities had overstepped their agreed defence quotas in guns and infantry, there was the revocation of the Edict of Nantes in 1685. This gave the country's ruling elite authority for invasion and eviction. Thousands of Frenchmen and women arrived in South Africa when they could not stand their own country any more, bringing with them their most useful abilities. They knew how to grow the vine and to make wine, something very useful in a land that is so dry during the months of June to September. The farmers already settled in the country were clever. They did not want all sorts of different European languages being used throughout South Africa, so they settled these newcomers in widely different areas of this extensive country. The result was that in two generations the descendants of the original immigrants had lost the language of the 'old country' and were speaking the Dutch-Afrikaans speech like everyone else of European origin. That's how many names even nowadays are really French, like Terreblanche, Visagie, de Villiers, du Toit and many others, and they even look like Frenchmen and women, but they have no connection whatsoever with the old country of brandy, champagne, camemberts, frogs' legs, snails and public urination.

Many French people also left their old country one century later following the warning by King Louis XV, 'Après moi le déluge', translated as 'After me the flood' or 'The shower is after me', which these émigrés took seriously. Hence they avoided the revenge of the revolutionaries and the cutting edge of the guillotine. They did not stop, however, in South Africa, but continued eastwards to populate the islands of La Réunion and Mauritius, where their descendants still speak the language of France; a rather more agreeable one than that rough guttural language called Afrikaans.

It can be said that nowadays most white ex-Europeans of South Africa are friendly on first meeting each other, unless there are reasons to be otherwise, and this friendship is reinforced by many sports and evening entertainments common to gregarious communities. More especially is this true in country places where the country club is a great meeting place for general social intercourse, rather more so than in big cities where spontaneous friendships are not so easily established.

One such place was the village of Crompton with its fine country clubhouse with a shoulder-high brick wall and thick thatching reaching two storeys high, supported by thick black beams soaked in creosote to discourage the termites. It was now twenty years old, having been built to replace the old one that dated to one hundred years before. There were many stories of the past to regale newcomers – events of importance and amusements as told by old timers and raconteurs.

One such story was the famous cricket match in 1975 between the landed gentry and the artisans of the village. The landowners nearly always won, probably because of their better education at expensive schools where batting, bowling and fielding were given prominence over such mundane matters as making a living and establishing girlfriends. During one match, the score stood at 88 all out for the artisans. The gentry were 75 for 8; could they make the 14 runs needed? Then the gentry's side reached 87 runs for 9 wickets. Would they get the two runs to beat the artisans of Crompton once more as in the last fifteen years? The bowler, Harry Benson, manager of the local garage, with a fixed determined look at the middle stump twenty-two yards away and more, was running down the field intent on clean bowling young George Ponsonby, owner of four thousand acres of prime land with the best dairy herd in the country, supplying four thousand gallons of milk daily to the town of Durban, thirty-five kilometres away. As Harry was hurtling down ready to cast a ball at one hundred kilometres an hour, a great hue and cry arose from the spectators and the barman roared in his stentorian voice, 'The grass in the parking lot is on fire; there's a grass fire where the cars are parked.'

George Ponsonby, catching the tone of fear and warning in the loud cries, looked quickly at the cars parked in the paddock normally used for grazing, now a field with a carpet of straw; so long ago had there been the last rainfall. Was his Mercedes Benz safe? At the same time, the ball struck sharply the middle stump; the tenth batsman was clean bowled.

As George raced to the cars, he shouted to Harry, 'That is not fair; unfair interference from outside.'

Meanwhile Harry was dancing with delight. The artisans had won at last; the danger to the cars could wait half a minute. In fact, there were so many people converging upon their cars to drive away quickly from the flaming dry grass and flying embers that there was no interest in discussing any fairness or unfairness. Most of the cars were saved; a few were stuck, the owners away visiting farms next door with old school friends in the dairy and cattle business. But the danger did not stop there. The barman went frantic as embers were driven on to the thick thatching of the clubhouse, while elsewhere the fire threatened the borders, grass tennis courts, the bowling green, golf course and outhouses. He yelled for two assistants to climb up the ladders on to the roof, each carrying four bottles of beer in hands and in pockets. During this time of drought, there was no water to spare. They shook the pint bottles and squirted the smouldering embers on the thatching blown there by the wind. At the same time, the barman exhorted all the men to drink all the beer they could and to piss on anything burning. 'Don't waste your urine,' he kept shouting as he went on squirting beer at smoking spots on the thatched roof. The whole male company took part willingly; and of course the women helped by supplying and advising. So they went on squirting or pissing on everything that was in flames. In an hour, the watering party was successful; the clubhouse was saved; only the grounds and outhouses had been seared in places.

Another memorable occasion was when the visiting tennis team from Paris came to play Crompton's players during the month of December – holiday time for students and teachers; post-calving time for farmers. It was an enjoyable time full of shrieks and laughs as the Crompton men players powered their way to victory, being stronger and more athletic. The French women's team managed to win their games, being more agile than the Crompton ladies, who were all wives and mothers. The Frenchmen had no chance in their singles and the mixed doubles matches, being less fit and mobile than the farmers of Crompton.

After the tennis matches, the men all enjoyed a cooling shower, but the club's president apologised profusely to the French ladies that there were no women's showers.

'They still have to be built,' he explained. 'What you can do is visit the houses nearby for a quick wash and shower with our lady members'.

The Frenchwomen were not having that!

'Ven zee men 'ave finished, ve will use zeir facilities, and ask zem to 'urry up.'

The president was aghast and against this arrangement, which was contrary to the rules and decorum of the club, or any club of its kind for that matter. When the men were finishing drying off, the women simply moved in, stripped and enjoyed a short cooling shower, since there was no drought at that time. The men were highly amused, for they considered the men's toilet area as their own private property and precinct. They came up to the Gallic ladies with their cocks hanging out saying, 'How about this one? Do you fancy this one?'

The women were not bothered at all. One, Françoise Durand, simply answered to their surprise, 'Love eez not just a cock in a 'ole, love eez much more of zee feelings and zee affections of two people; you 'ave a lot to learn; it is lovely in zee cold vater; now vee go and ye talk of tings friendly.'

So that evening was made for posterity and memories with the adage, 'Love eez not just a cock in a 'ole. Vive la différence.'

Marius's Studies

Marius Wessels was a follower of Johannes Venter with a difference. He had a passion for learning, was unfettered by prejudice, had unlimited funds and was intent on knowing what other men knew. It was Marius Wessels who started the investigations into anti-state activities. All thoughts and intentions meant to reduce government and police strength and subvert policy were considered anti-state activities. There was lots of scope, a whole range of human activities, which were put down and labelled as Anti-Government Actions, known as AGAs. The most common ones were those tending to undermine the system of apartheid.

It was hard for those placed in between, like children of mixed parentage, those with an African mother and a German father, for instance; such examples were accommodated as exceptions to the rule of separateness. The Cape coloureds constituted such an exception; they were neither black Africans nor white settlers. They were a people on their own, with their own ways of earning, living and loving. There was the example of a Mr Dunn, a fertile Scotsman who had lived during the previous century and acquired himself forty Zulu wives. His children had numbered two hundred, all accepted as members of the British Zulu colony in the province of Natal. One hundred years later, it was not known how numerous his grandchildren and great-grandchildren were. Most of these had lost the language of their eminent grandfather, to the point of not even speaking English, but they were often distinguished by their physique.

There were examples of unfortunate shipwrecked people lost on distant shores where rescue was impossible during the eighteenth and nineteenth centuries. Such people numbered a mere handful. The men were massacred; the poor women kept in captivity as slaves and used for procreation. Their numbers fade into insignificance when compared with the millions and millions of unfortunate blacks who were captured and shipped in the most cruel way to work the fields of cotton and sugar cane across the Atlantic. Their offspring later made for a mixed people who soon lost their mother tongue and, say, two generations later, did not know quite who they were.

Marius was not concerned with these fringe examples of 'in betweens'. His interest was in the purity and strength of his country of Polygonia. The Asiatics who had been brought over in the last century were likewise a people whom Marius considered to be a people apart. They had come to work in the sugar cane fields and a century later they were traders, businessmen and many professionals. They numbered around one million – Hindus, Mohammedans, Gujaratis, Tamils, Telugus, Punjabis, Dravidians.

Marius Wessels was concerned with the strength and unity of his people in relation to the very much greater African tribal population of the whole country. His objective was the maintenance of the strong white race of his European antecedents, the people with the mission of God's revelation to his God-fearing people. They had been sent to this strange land to develop and regulate its resources for the benefit of those living there as well as to help all the many others north of South Africa, and God knows how many of them needed help. There was the example of the Congo in 1960, when thousands travelled south to avoid their country's civil war; likewise, there were thousands of refugees from Mozambique and Angola, where different warring fictions were more interested in inflicting military success than in the occupation of land and cattle ranching and farming. There were many other examples of refugees, as when people moving over hundreds of kilometres to try to find better conditions and ended up starving in semi-desert areas; and it was most often the help and care from South Africa that rescued these people. These examples showed to Marius Wessels the special place he and his people held and intended to go on holding. He insisted on the sacred mission of national security and those who tried to endanger this security were condemned as unpatriotic, anti-national and, finally, communist traitors who followed a course of action under the directions of another country for another set of leaders and for the benefit of another country: what could be more traitorous?

It was Marius Wessels who insisted during the 1960s that the communist influence in his country was considerably more extensive and dangerous than most people had previously suspected. There were various acts of disobedience that he found suspicious, together with outright organised crowd violence, leaving many people injured and achieving nothing but annoyance among several groups of people. Marius's studies had not been superficial. After the LLB degree acquired from Durban University, he had done legal studies at Oxford University, postgraduate work in international law, mercantile law, constitutional law, and finished off with the spirit of the law, considering the law as justice in itself rather than a comparison of judgements made from a conjunction of legal examples.

Marius was hoping that reason and knowledge, together with experience and common sense, would provide the guiding influence for correct procedure in his work for the future. By this it can be seen that he was not a sceptic nor a sadist, but a reasonable and an intellectual optimist.

More Studies

Further than that, however, Marius Wessels, who spent three years in England doing postgraduate studies, became intensely interested in Europe itself. There were seventeen countries of consequence in Europe, leaving out such small and unimportant principalities as Monte Carlo, San Marino, Andorra and Liechtenstein. Each had rather different languages, but there was something special about the people. They were not just white Europeans, but were purposive in their behaviour, whether they were capitalists, artisans, proletarians or simply common criminals. There was a decided purposefulness about their make-up which was somehow different from those of other people he had met from many other places. He could not ignore their interesting qualities and so, to cap his many studies in law he decided to do a crash course in European history.

He learned about Egyptian civilisation – admittedly not European, but it was a good place at which to start – then the so-called Classical age of the Greeks and Romans, the Dark Ages, the Middle Ages, the Renaissance, the Age of Enlightenment, the Age of Reason, the Industrial Revolution; then Democracy, Imperialism and the colonial rush for overseas possessions; then finally the present age of enlightened technology, with its recent memories of wars, massacres, holocausts and disasters.

Marius Wessels, after all these studies, could not help wondering what was successful and praiseworthy, and being a God-fearing man, he started to wonder where was goodness to be found on this earth of ours. He came to understand such factors as genetic influences, conditioned-communal reflexes, the historic pre-conscience and social determinism, all couched in terms well established by sociologists and law-makers. He decided that the right thing for him to do was to go back to his country and work to guide his country in a direction that was both worthwhile and necessary.

That is why, when he returned to South Africa after an absence of five years, he was bent on preserving what he considered as really and truly valuable.

After two years in a magistrate's court, judging petty crime and larceny, felonies and even murders that he referred to the Supreme Court, he was soon appointed an administrator in the provincial National Party as a legal adviser, and then, later, Minister of Internal Security. With his flair for understanding the human condition, his extensive understanding of law in its many different aspects and his love for his country, he was in fact the best man for this post as Minister of Internal Security. Furthermore, he claimed a kind of dominance by virtue of European abilities; he claimed the whites were in the vanguard of progress because of their results in developments both in the arts and the sciences, in discoveries as in inventions, in exploration and in technology. He acknowledged the awful disasters of the immoral ideologies; the massacres by the Nazi regime in the name of German progress and superiority; likewise the horrible examples among the international socialists of the USSR, where millions were killed in the name and for the sake of socialist stability and of progress. These examples he acknowledged as a terrible distortion of authentic values among a civilised people, which was highly regrettable and to be avoided in the course of human affairs.

Marius went so far as to state his opinion that it was large, strong, socialist organisations that had ruined the world during the latter two-thirds of the century. There was the example of National Socialism in Germany. In six years, it had raised Germany from dire poverty and weakness, making it into such a strong country that it had been able to invade the rest of Europe; but then it had ruined it for the next ten years. They were stopped by the Russian winters and Soviet socialists, who then, in their turn, had proceeded to ruin their country with experiments in enforced socialism resulting in millions of deaths and, with Germany defeated, had proceeded to deal out death throughout the world with their distribution of arms and ammunition, grenades and landmines to every country that wished for revolution, violence and massacres in the name of progress.

Marius used to say, 'Socialism has become the curse of this century.' He admitted that socialists were able to make a marvellous contribution in small groups pressing for improved salary scales, arranged medical and pension schemes, care for the aged and the infirm, protection against industrial accidents and petty strikes and so on. But once they become a national force, they become a mortal menace. And that is what he was up against in South Africa. The poor and helpless were promised help and support. They were given teaching, arms and promises. And what happened? They became rebels against the established authorities as well as vengeful against their old foes of many years using the arms and ammunition which they could not have afforded to pay for themselves. 'This is the curse of socialism,' he used to say and went on further in predicting a return to the Dark Ages, with the loss of the values of the old civilisation, culminating in force as the final arbiter.

Even with the younger generation, Marius used to say that one could see a loss of strength with the increasing divorce rate, and the increase in drug abuse and alcoholism; and just to watch modern dancing was enough to disgust anyone of his generation, the way they indulged in drumbeat factory-noise music, with a drumbeat ritual rhythm, not even touching one another, as if in preparation for some cannibalistic feast.

He cited the example of sport. It was marvellous to see so many indulging in active energetic sport, but, as far as Marius was concerned, it did not matter a tittle or a jot who won in matches and competitions, though he was glad when his own country's teams won. What was important was that there were so many who kept up strong, fine, energetic, lively, healthy physiques, together with a healthy social life. That was the really important result. And just what would be the alternative if these millions were not indulging in these energetic exercises? They would be indulging in drink, tobacco or drugs, or else chasing other people's women, or worse, going for political involvement with ideas of conspiracy, confrontation and even violence in the name and for the sake of some political party whose aims and ideas were considered superior to those of others.

Marius's Ambitions

Marius Wessels's criticism did not stop there. Marius used to say that while millions were keeping up their strength with worthwhile exercises and games, how many more millions were wasting theirs while watching thousands of matches throughout the world? They became wildly excited over the success of their favourite teams or indulged in miserable recriminations if their favourite sides did not come out as victors.

'Just imagine,' Marius used to say, 'how interesting it would be if once a month a busload of sport fans went up to a mountain or large hill; there are so many hills and mountains that are quite bare of trees, whereas a hundred years ago all these bare geographical features were covered with trees and bushes, as shown by paintings of that time. Once a month, a busload of sport and nature enthusiasts could venture up to these sadly diminished, denuded mountains and start reafforestation with saplings and seeds. The programme could be called something like "Adopt a hill or mountain and try reafforestation". Instead of sitting and watching other people playing games, matches and competitions; week after week, they would be exhorted with statements like "Make your country green again as it was a century ago".' Such was the enthusiasm he had for his country that Marius would propagate these ideas as often as he found a suitable occasion.

It was while Marius was giving a talk at the aforementioned village of Crompton that he met the enthusiastic and gregarious people of the village who were most interested in his talk called 'Security and Harmony'. This was all about the value of cooperation and anti-pollution endeavours, mixed up with the need for soil conservation, plus the great idea of trying the worthwhile programme for promoting the growth of indigenous trees of the country.

During Marius's first talk to Crompton, he described how there were many trees suitable for any tree-growing project in the country. As an example, there's the mopane butterfly tree which grows well in alluvial soil and makes good wood for furniture. The weeping boerboom or tree fuchsia is a lovely tree for shade and colours, with rich red leaves with scarlet fuchsia-like flowers on its stem. The Cape ash (essenhout) gives much shade with a mahogany-like wood and is useful in that it grows particularly well and fast in sandy soil. The kaffirboom or lucky bean tree grows well in coastal areas and along streams, with thorny branches and orange scarlet flowers that appear before the leaves develop. The umbrella thorn tree (haak-en-steek) of the acacia family, the curse of parachutists, is usually a short ten to twenty-five foot tree with a spreading flat top of branches with long thorns and a profusion of yellow or white flowers, ideal for hilltops as a hardy and drought-resistant tree, though slow growing. Then there's the waterberry (waterhout), an evergreen shady tree with thick dark green leaves, which does well in open grasslands as well as by wet forests; a relative of the eucalyptus gum tree found in Australia.

These are just some of the species of trees that Marius took an interest in, among the many dozens and dozens of varieties that might possibly be planted and grown by nature enthusiasts.

'Hopefully, some sport enthusiasts also might take off on a Saturday, perhaps once a month or so, to try covering some of our bare hills and mountains with as much enthusiasm as they do in following their favourite teams,' Marius would declare, 'as these teams chase a bag of wind across sports fields for the sake of some sporting glory.'

During the break between talks and questions, he was entertained with a clubhouse supper, a standing finger supper, when he was happy to meet and get acquainted with a charming farmer's daughter called Brenda Brannigan, who spoke good English, but was more fluent in Afrikaans. Her name was evocative of her Irish origin, which stemmed from her father's grandfather. This ancestor – 'old man Patrick' as he was always referred to – had left his native Ireland at the end of the last century, coming from Tipperary, or was it Limerick; it could never be remembered for sure which town it had been. He had come to join up with the armed forces in the Boer War to get a chance of fighting the

English who had been occupying his own country for six centuries, against whom the inhabitants had been powerless since they were poorly armed while the British were strongly garrisoned all over the green land of Erin. Fortunately for him, old man Patrick had only taken part in the siege of Ladysmith, had been wounded in the leg, then convalesced for six months during the time it takes for a smashed femur to repair.

More significant had been his discharge and settlement on two thousand acres of land suitable for cattle and maize farming, bought using his army pay plus funds saved while working for three years as assistant manager with cattle, winter wheat and mealies. That had been a useful experience for him, since this country's farming techniques vary considerably from those in Ireland. The farm was quite near to the village of Crompton, which he never left again except for one visit to his old home town in Ireland after a set of good harvests. This allowed him four months' absence from the farm while his second son took over its management. The first son was not cut out for farm management. He had joined the police and then made his career the army.

Marius was delighted to meet such a sweet person as Brenda, with her slightly dumpy figure and a sweet smile of peace, looking most attractive in a sweater which showed off her burgeoning femininity to advantage. He admired her comely homely manner that put her at ease in company, either with friends or with newly met strangers. She had trained as an infant schoolteacher with a diploma which allowed her to teach children up to the age of seven or eight, and she was most capable in doing just that; an important time in a child's education.

She admired him for qualities she had always hoped to find in a man and a friend, the qualities of intelligence and loquacity, combined with a caring attitude. She did not care much for silent men whom others called the strong silent sort; she saw them as a weak, silent kind. His ability as a speaker was obvious. The other qualities she admired were also patently evident in Marius Wessels.

After Marius and his companion Jarpy Visagie had had a couple of dops in the men's bar and had met some of the male residents of Crompton, they were just leaving to join the crowd at the finger supper arranged for them when he saw Brenda standing in the doorway of the ladies' bar with the light shining behind her and framing her head in a glow of light that struck Marius with wonder and admiration. And such a sensible hairstyle too – straight, chocolate brown hair that stopped short at mid-neck level, thought Marius. Not like that other woman at a previous club meeting in Consort who had kissed him enthusiastically with loose tresses swirling around her as she kissed him with fervour on the forehead, she being slightly taller than himself. Her hair had blown into his face, nose, eyes and neck causing him to sneeze all over her left bosom, a fact that caused him more embarrassment than his admirer.

Brenda blurted out how interesting and engaging she had found his talk.

'So glad you have this interest in trees. Would you care to have a quick look around the club grounds where my younger brother Billy and I have been taking a great interest in the planting of trees? And Billy has such green fingers,' she added. 'He prepares the holes himself with wood chips and compost manure at the bottom for the young trees, and they always grow so well.'

So they took a quick look to admire avocado pear trees, a couple of litchis, a mango, several lemon trees for the gin-and-tonic drinkers, the sausage tree with its velvety crimson flowers and many others. Brenda led the way through the side door of the clubhouse, holding him lightly by the forearm to avoid drainage holes and uneven paths outside the kitchen area. This set Marius singing a snatch of a song from a musical, 'The Boy Friend', as they strolled to the club gardens:

Hold my hand, I'm a strange-looking parasite,
All lost in the undergrowth, a strange looking parasite.

This sent Brenda into fits of giggles and laughter, which soon had Marius also laughing. Of course, with his Dutch background and her Irish one and their mutual dislike for the *rooinek*, the country's nickname for the English, their acquaintance soon turned into a friendship, thence to a romance and finished as a partnership with vows 'to have and to hold, for better or worse, till death do us part', that indeed did last for a lifetime.

He was delighted later to be presented with four and a half children; three sons and a daughter, the same as Brenda and her three brothers. The half child was a miscarriage at six months, much later on, identified as a female. Marius was truly compassionate, like all caring fathers. Brenda named her Moira, the Greek for 'fate', in her imagination, and sometimes wondered how she might have turned out if fate had been kinder.

What Mr Wessels wished for was a strong country led by a united people who could contain the masses and keep them satisfied. His argument was, 'We are the best people to rule and reign; without us, the country would go to rack and ruin.' So, to implement this, he encouraged a special Secret Service, a strong police force and stronger armed forces, run by whites of European descent, recent or several generations back, with qualities of reliability, trust and honesty. There were blacks used in these services, certainly as cleaners, servers and messenger boys. These were menial tasks, but he considered that that was where they belonged. If there were some whites who were delinquent, unreliable and lacking in honesty, that was regrettable and they were kept at a status slightly above cleaners, servers and messengers.

So while Marius's strong organisations were well established and diligent for national preservation, other groups were growing, mostly outside but also inside the country, with their own influences among elements in the villages and towns.

The Store

Joseph Khuzwayo was told to 'get on with it', and to start the development of his own groups. This instruction came to him from the director of the South African Democratic Front, which country they called Polygonia among themselves. Their head-quarters were situated in London at number 14 Blackwell Street, Hackney. There they received émigrés who had left their homes because of political or legal injustice, or worse, because of life threats to their lives, loss of dear ones and near ones, or even because there was no longer employment once their revolutionary aims were known. The chance of overseas employment and even partnership was better than unemployment in South Africa, with the shame and embarrassment of depending of friends and relatives and no hope of repaying them. These people's main hope in London, or anywhere else in the world, while they were living out their lives as émigrés, was one day to be able to return to the land of their birth and schooling, where they felt that they still belonged.

But before Joseph could start any serious project and pro-gramme of his own at his village together with influencing and teaching others, he as a leader and teacher had to go through an initiation process that was most important. It was a programme that would make him a man instead of being constantly a boy. It was a programme of cutting, together with personal growth, that would make him a man by virtue of being circumcised; the *Ukusoka*, also known as the *Ukoluka* among other people. This was the tradition of the land where he lived.

So it was arranged that he left with a group numbering four-teen in all; he was a *Umkhwetha* with the others, known collectively as *Abakhwetha*, who left to go to a nearby grove alongside the river, where they were housed in huts made of wattle branches and leaves covered with thatching and more branches. It was a shelter where they were to live for the two to

four weeks during the time that it takes to recover from the
important wound of circumcision. The day after settling into their
new temporary shelter, the cutter of foreskins, the *Ingcibi* was
there with his sharp assegai, plus a wood block placed in the
centre of the area beside a tent. Each *Umkhwetha* was told to strip
and bathe in the nearby cool pool to get himself clean and to
ensure a smallness of genital tissues. Then the cutter snipped off
each boy's superfluous skin; held over the wooden block and with
the sharp assegai, each boy had had his cut, all of them in a matter
of fifteen minutes. The wound was immediately dressed with
leaves of the Ixubani tree, wrapped with thread and secured with a
leather strap to keep the whole organ intact within and protected.

After this minor surgery, the *Ingcibi* cutter left promptly to go
to another far-off place for a similar performance, never to be
seen again. Some of the boys bled profusely. Others were lucky
with only a minor haemorrhage.

In one week, some had had a successful healing, others needed
dressings for two weeks. Joseph was lucky. In ten days, his
reproductive organ was healed and he was ready for dismissal.
During that whole period, they had smeared themselves with a
whitish clay over face and body to show anyone in sight that they
were going through a purification process. The man who cared
for them, the *Ikhankatha*, would dress the wounds daily, and small
boys brought them food with small drinks three times daily, but
no meat during that time. It was an experience which changed the
boys into men. After this dermal excision, they would be considered as men with authority. They were no longer bearers of
hidden diseases.

They were both clean and enhanced with a new authority.
And these men, now evolved into serious manhood, were ready to
face their future with the strength of authority which was far
more significant than their previous status had allowed. This band
of men were bound in a brotherhood, a foreskin brotherhood
which would last them for their lifetime. Those who missed this
programme were considered boys for their entire lives. Those
who went to a government hospital or a mission one were
considered as not having had the real thing for the promotion to
manhood. They were like girls, it was said, not having suffered

and lacking *Abakhwetha* comrades.

It was also a fact that women of their race demanded that husbands should have had a *Ukusoka* or a *Ukoluka* completed before marriage. This was imperative as a token of a safe and serious marriage. Some tribes went so far as to indulge in the circumcision of their girls; the excision of the clitoris left a scarred area in the pubic region insensitive to the sexual act, and so rendered them faithful to their husbands, or so it was taught.

After this period of a few weeks, Joseph was able and ready to start at Esigodeni with a small store at the village outskirts, not far from the new post office. This is where his poor unfortunate cachectic and withered father had had two acres of land to himself as a result of the chief's magnanimity following the father's gift of five hundred rand, saved during his five years of mining. This land had enabled the family to grow maize, about fourteen bags yearly. They also had had two cows, each giving a calf every two years, and milk thereafter for nine months, if there were not too many ticks; plus a flock of goats, one of which was culled every three months for the family stew pot, using the communal grazing ground.

These two acres had helped the family along together with the added bonanza of each girl's *lobola*. This was the marriage price each sister received from her new husband-to-be. The *lobola* was calculated according to the value of each daughter, as estimated at the age of seventeen or over. They had reached standard four at school at the age of twelve and then left school, which meant they could read and write in Zulu; they had five hundred words of English and this other language, Afrikaans; knew the rudiments of hygiene; had vague ideas about geography and history, and were up to elementary arithmetic. That put their value at around two thousand rand each, payable with cows, each averaging five hundred rand in value or its equivalent such as money, gold ornaments and household effects.

The small store that old man Phineas had started when he was mobile was really a shack rather than a store and had been used as a shed for tools and a place from which he had sold quart beers at two rand each plus cool drinks, Coke and orangeade or lemonade that were kept in a deep trench in the shack next to their home for coolness for friends and acquaintances. This had allowed him to make a small profit, which become easier as the children grew up since they were able to go to the village forty kilometres away to stock up with drinks every two or three weeks. This small trade had made quite a difference to the household. Before they had subsisted; now they lived with the assurance of a steady livelihood. Before they used to worry about the next week's, and even the next day's, food supply. Now they were sure of meat, bread, margarine and eggs daily.

But it meant having someone at the store all the time, and not only during the day, but also at night when one of the family had to be present with their faithful dog, an Alsatian bitch named Josephine, unless the small store was empty of stock. These night precautions stopped the occasional break-ins where stock of up to a hundred rand might easily have been stolen, with no hope of redress or even of recapture; making a charge at the local police station charge office was of no avail.

For Joseph Khuzwayo, this buying and selling was therefore not a new experience. When twelve years old, he would buy a crate of beer, quart size, twelve quarts per crate, for one rand fifty per quart. They were sold at two rand each to make a profit of six rand. But each empty bottle cost fifty cents, hence, six rand for the empties in a crate, and the crate cost two rand. Joseph needed a down payment of twenty-six rand, or eighteen rand with all the empties in hand, to make a profit of six rand. With twenty-six rand in hand before buying, it was easy to yield to temptation to get an ice cream, buns with jam, or a Bunny Chow – half a loaf with curried mincemeat inside, very nourishing, especially during the cold days when hunger and cold made strong demands on him or his sisters, Umuhle, Ntombi and Ntombifuthi – but, of course, this would leave them without any capital for investing in these drinks. In fact they did this once, returning home short of one crate to face the wrath of their father who shouted and abused them for this short-sighted action to give themselves a few hours' pleasure, but deny the family a six rand profit over the coming days. This was a lesson they never were to forget: suffer hunger now, but survive to be able to carry on with all the family for just another few days.

Another problem was that the liquor store was forty kilometres away, and they only took back a crate when filled with twelve empty bottles. Many times the empty bottles did not return after being sold, and they might be left with sixteen bottles and two empty crates. They started 'operation empty bottles'. This involved scrounging in dustbins, behind garages and local shebeens, and in town in similar localities. They made the surprising discovery that, by careful searching, they were able to collect many more empty bottles than needed for two crates. There were pint bottles giving ten cents each, and tin cans giving at the town scrapyard fifteen cents per kilogram plus the fifty cents for the extra big quart bottles as singles, over and above those in the crates. The question of transport to the town was solved by Samuel Mthembu, an old school friend of their father, who owned and ran a one-pump hand-operated petrol station and did car repairs. He would tell the children, though they were not children any more but young adults, 'I'll be going into the big city tomorrow, eleven o'clock, ntambani.' Then two of them would sit at the back of the truck, usually with two crates of empty beer bottles, two sacks of pint bottles, three sacks of crushed tins and a few smaller bags of empty quart bottles, every two to three weeks, to return with two crates of full quart bottles in Samuel's bumbling truck or by public bus service at one rand each, to arrive just at twilight at 6 p.m., in time for home, *putu* and beans, and an early sleep.

These experiences taught these young people the value of money and the value of thrift together with an understanding of the economics of trade. These experiences were to be most useful for Joseph in the years to come.

The Store's Beginning

After this political training in Tanzania, Joseph Khuzwayo was faced with a family group at his village of his ageing mother, Jabulile, who was glad he had qualified in whatever it was he had gone to study. She never quite knew nor understood what it was he had studied, but she realised it wasn't the same programme that other young men went through, for when they came back they were such clever speakers at their local church. But Joseph never went to the local church to speak at the speaker's desk. Joseph assured old Mrs Lily Jabulile Khuzwayo that he had gone to receive training for the good of his country. Old mother Khuzwayo assured him that she wanted only the good of the family group and the good of the people of the village; never mind the country. Her country was the village of Esigodeni; outside Esigodeni was the problem of someone else. Joseph tried to assure her he would try for the good of the country and the village; the former would come to include the latter in parallel with the extent of his influence and successes.

The family circle now consisted of the last sister, Ntombi-futhi, Joseph and grandmother gogo Jabulile, who had still not met up with the new grandson that she knew about and was keen to be acquainted with. The last *lobola* for the second daughter, Ntombi, had been used; four hundred rand to buy a large armchair with broad armrests for the matriarch Khuzwayo; some of the rest to establish a small store at the corner of the field where the young ones had sold beer a few years before; the balance of the cash, five hundred rand, went to the local *induna*, the head man, to obtain permission to restart the small store at the same place where Phineas had started the small drinks store, from where the children had continued selling until Joseph's departure.

So Joseph bought up planks, a hammer and saw, long nails and old corrugated iron sheet roofing to set up this bigger store plus supplies. Joseph, quite bossy now, assured them that it did not matter if they went into debt. Once their business was going, it was sure to be profitable because – and here he embellished his argument – of an increased population by virtue of better medical services with its good programme and the cure of many diseases among the young and old. Furthermore, a new factory up the hill was making cement from the heavy clay in the area and a new national road was in the making only two kilometres away. All this sounded convincing enough, and it turned out to be exactly as he had predicted. There had occurred a significant increase in the local population.

The store was opened within one week of placing the upright tar-soaked poles and the placing of the first plank. It was not difficult to arrange one counter with storage space behind, one spare room nearby for more storage with one back door and a front door for easy access for service and supplies with a roof over the lot.

The occasion was marked with a feast for family and friends. A calf was killed, born of the *lobola* cow of two years before. This was roasted nearby, served with *putu* porridge and a relish of vegetables – spinach, dandelion leaves, young nettle shoots with beans. It was a bean feast to please all palates. Joseph gave a speech after the removal of a sheet in front of the counter, rather as if it were an opening ceremony like that he had seen on a grander style in film he'd watched some time before while at Camp Kosi. There was also a prayer to the ancestors to plead for their help and power in providing success in this family business and a further prayer to the God of the universe who takes an interest in human affairs. It was over in one day; a good feast was had by all and all promised allegiance in commerce to the Khuzwayo family, giving them preference in trade in the area.

The store went from being a poor trading centre to a fairly busy one. The place was often strewn with empty food tins, plastics and papers. The grass field became a muck area during the rainy season and a paraffin fridge had been found and installed for the cold drinks, which until then had only been cold by virtue of an earthen cellar dug in a corner of the spare room. From the time of the paraffin fridge, trade increased noticeably. Workers stopped by for a really cold Coke, Fanta or beers on weekdays or weekends. A daily supply of twelve loaves was established, except on Sundays. A gas stove was included for cooking sausages and curried mince, and for tea and coffee. The bread was never sold out except at weekends, when there was never enough. The family had leftovers as their necessary fare, plenty on weekdays and rather short at weekends, something they had never known before. By then there were another two employees, Nonhlanhla to help with kitchen duties, sales, and food displays, and Wandile to help with store removals, opening of boxes, store movements from shops to truck, hired for the purpose at the store, and also for the handling of money matters once he had proved himself as reliable and trustworthy.

It was then that safeguarding of finances become serious. Money left in the store was stolen twice during the night when the Alsatian bitch was enticed from her duties while on heat by another ardent Alsatian dog. While the animals chased around, a third party had entered, stolen the money and left, all in the space of twenty seconds; obviously they were men who knew the layout of the premises. Several pleas by Joseph for a bank at Esigodeni resulted in the one-day-a-week opening of Folks Bank on a Wednesday morning, which meant every Tuesday night was target night. The money was secured by the owner with all paper money screwed tightly up into a cigar tin container and kept up his anus and released the next day by the use of a purgative. The rest of the money in coins was kept in a cloth bag under grandma's left breast, though she did not always know it. The store slowly prospered; another room was added with a strength-ened roof; entry through the roof was the usual way for thieves to get inside.

This was when Joseph received his second message from the International Polygonian Democratic Front in code. Decoded it read, 'What are you doing for your country?'

At that time of the party's development, couriers used the simple code of writing a Z for an A, a Y for a B, and so on. So what Joseph had received was a message which said, 'Dszg ziv blf wlrms uli blfi xlfngib?' which he was able to decode in two minutes. Anyone else finding such a jumble of letters might have taken half an hour to decipher it, and should there have been any urgency, it would have given the courier time to escape, though in this case there was no special secret or mystery involved. It was just that the men continued using the code as ordered by their directors, probably as a means of maintaining familiarity with the code's use for when it would be important.

He replied in an English statement and returned it via the original messenger, known to his friends and others by the name Pedro, and by no other name except the epithet 'Pedro the Fisherman', because of his trade in fish.

Joseph's message said, 'I will do what I can when I can.'

Joseph's Store

Meanwhile back in the store, Joseph really did start using his influence seriously in group meetings. He started with men in the area, choosing eleven with whom to talk seriously in the jargon of early political science. This is our country, we are here because of our ancestors; this land belongs more to us than to anyone else; we must work together as if we were its owners, not its servants; power comes from unity as well as from property and financial backing. He would talk gravely, but never loudly as if he were fighting with the words. These meetings were held mostly as a friendly get-together, but he had to change this. Being friendly was not good enough. He enlisted the men as members of the local branch of the DDP, the Democratic Development of Polygonia, with names recorded in a small black notebook kept under the counter inside the cardboard box containing accounts and letters. Each person had a nickname to be used only at these meetings. Joseph took the name of Max, short for Maximillian, but chosen because of its resemblance to Karl Marx, their icon in politics and philosophy. There were Den, Bill, Xosh, Hal, Chas, Jolly, Pan, Gat, Tondo, Mick and Ken, each name relating to some quality of the person or his real name.

Over a year, the group met monthly, always with one or two missing, every first Tuesday of the month in the evening after the store closed at about 6 p.m., the end of the working day with a week's takings in hand and the day before the local bank opened. That way the money of the week was safe while the ten or eleven men were together after which it was hidden in the body spaces already mentioned.

Joseph had themes he developed with the help of a few books he was able to obtain through friends and the occasional visit to the town library at Iqubani, forty kilometres away. His English was now good enough to understand most of the literature in books, thanks to the local librarian, Mick, one of the twelve, who helped with difficult words and the use of dictionaries; first English to Zulu, then just English to English.

His main theme was still – this is our country and that of our fathers and the fathers of our fathers. We are the masters, not forever the servants, political progress comes through strife, the colonists came here from adventure and necessity; their homes were short of land, or work or just uninteresting. The new countries were open with a chance for work, enterprise, adventure. Progress was through a struggle of sorts; the old order was confronted with a new order; the strife made a change that was always an improvement, a step towards another system. Our old system was underdeveloped.

Another theme was their own need for a better education, especially for the young and adolescents. Those over fifty were considered as not being able to benefit from any special tuition. It was pathetic how many people never knew their age, their place of birth, or their grandparents' histories. An example was one Doris, daughter of Zipho, whose mother died in childbirth; Zipho, the father, was lost in the mines to the north in Johannesburg and was never seen again; he was probably Sotho in origin. Doris was cared for by the local church verger until she was ten years old, then by a gardener for the next fifty years. Doris was the village waif with no background, and she was just one example. There was Tandi, saved by the hospital from dysentery at the age of three, who returned home a month later when his two parents were dead, probably from typhoid. He was taken by the garage assistant's wife until he was seven, then used as a messenger boy and tool carrier. The villagers did not know his parents; they had been part-time workers on the cattle or maize farms and probably came from the next village. When Tandi was twelve years old, he visited the next village to try to trace his parents and relatives, but got nowhere. He did not know their names, and nor did anyone else.

With a better education in all the towns and villages, these sorts of difficulties would be much reduced; there would develop the necessary self-reliance that is so important among our people, which at that moment was often lacking. So Joseph would instruct at each of these meetings, just a few details on needed improvements at each group meeting.

Group Meetings

There were other needs Joseph described, emphasised and encouraged, including the need for decent work ethics. Workers should know their rights and their duties. It was necessary that they should have correct standing, status, respect, decent clothing, protection and instruction. The most important, he considered, was work satisfaction, if that were possible, and the right to workers' meetings, or the right to know their rights. There were a number of these 'needs' that Joseph used to expand on. Another need was the need to be able to communicate. It was not enough just to say, 'Yes, baas, no, baas.' One could not expect the baases or bosses to learn their language, apart from saying *sawubona*, *kunjani* or *wenzani*. Communication was the basis for trust, understanding and communal reinforcement.

'You will notice how quickly the other tribes who come to work here on the farms, garages or the big cement factory nearby, learn our language in a few months,' he used to say. 'In this way, we learn about each other and become friends, and that is how it should be. But you can't expect that from the baases. They will never become friends, but they can become confidants and if they are really decent "chaps", they might become known as Baba, our father figure. Well, with five hundred words one can make sense in a language; with two thousand words, there is established convivial meaningful sense. Therefore, we need to learn the words of the baas. Ten words a week and you've got a thousand words in two years and your fellow workers should help you; though looking at what we've got here, it's more a question of you helping them. The choice of language is up to you. English for many of the workers, sometimes Dutch-Afrikaans, or German, or Italian, but I say English is the language to go for.'

Another theme of Joseph's instruction was Zulu home care. This was already well established by tradition and had been practised for many centuries. The toilets were at least fifty yards from the huts of the village. Water for washing was collected from the local well, the river or from a communal tap. Washing water was left overnight to encourage morning tooth brushing, hand and face washing and there was the weekly total body wash. All water for food was boiled as in soups, tea, coffee or other food preparations. No perishables were to be kept in the huts overnight except in freezing weather. This meant correct food allocation during the day to allow for total consumption. The next day the matriarch of the family with her daughters and daughters-in-law should cook enough for that day's consumption.

Another big problem was house care. Many hut dwellers feared thunderbolts coming through their wet thatching after rains during an electric storm. Sometimes whole families were killed inside such a hut when struck by lightning, or if not all of them, at least quite a few. That was a reason why so many trees were cut down near the huts. One hundred years ago all the bare hills that we see around us were covered with trees and shrubs; now you see bare hills. It was feared that thunderbolts would be drawn to the trees and the wet thatched roofs nearby. Joseph appealed for the need to grow trees and for lightning conductors on huts.

This meant using sizeable iron wires from a hut's top to the earth at the side of the hut to conduct the lightning bolt through the iron and so save the hut and all those inside. Some of the group stated there was no electric supply in the huts to work any electric conductor. Joseph had to explain that it was not necessary to have an electric supply to work an electric conductor. The conductor worked by virtue of its leading from the hut top to the ground; once struck, it usually burnt out and had to be replaced, but this would occur perhaps once in a lifetime.

Another home care addition encouraged was the construction of a chimney inside huts to ensure ventilation and clean air inside. It was well known that during winter, home fires inside huts made for smoke-filled homes that produced coughing and bronchitis, really nasty for the children of the family. Joseph explained that Zulus were clever and capable of weaving dresses, mats, hut thatching, hats, baskets and bracelets. It was an easy matter to make a woven piping arrangement above the fire place and grate in the hut's roof Many complained this was a new innovation, quite against the ideas and traditions of the fathers of the land. Joseph Khuzwayo insisted that some innovations were needed. The fathers of the land did not have the understanding nor did they comprehend their world as they did now. They must keep the good traditions and add to them further ways which are for their good. He never succeeded in convincing them of the use and effective need of such a new contraption. Those who tried said the chimneys fell off during high winds, or became clogged with the thatching it was made of. As for lightning conductors, Joseph explained how they were to be installed and encouraged their use, but the ordinary rural people mocked them as a sort of practice in witchcraft.

But Joseph persisted. Don't cut down trees uselessly; plant more trees, install lightning conductors; fashion a chimney in the hut roofs; all these changes are for the good of the people. All could take an interest in the stars and space travel, but their needs were around them, they ignored them at their peril. (Here he was quoting from Plato without knowing it.) His persistence in these matters gave him the nickname 'the chimney conductor', an epithet which was to give the secret police many months of confusion in the years to come.

Another big theme he was to propound was one started by his father many years before when Joseph was only eight years old or younger and whose memory he cherished. He had thought about and expanded upon the ideas his old man used to express. His father would say, 'We are black because our fathers were black, not just because God made us black. God made human beings thousands of years ago, and left nature to carry on. God started the process, nature fashioned the result. We are black because those who were not black died of skin diseases from the strong sun like ulcers, infections, and cancers, which we were spared. To be black is a positive quality; it is not only "Black is Beautiful", but black is strong, black is powerful, black is necessary. It is chemistry in our skin which relates to action and power that gives our skin this dark hue. Black is a positive fact of our being; we must be proud of our black skin. Black is more than beautiful; black is power. Hence black power by virtue of our possessions and ability, not black power through force and murder. The whites have power by their know-how, their scientific and social developments. When we have their know-how, then you will see they will become weak, feeble, and effete. That's when we will be recognised as black, beautiful and becoming the best.'

These were some of the themes Joseph lectured on during their monthly meeting. But lecturing never took longer than thirty minutes, for each meeting was also taken up with the last meeting's minutes, local news, party news, future projects and then one of his lectures. These would rotate over eighteen months then start again, by which time half the group were gone, through natural turnover. There were contacts every two years through party rallies and conventions. That's when many would call out to Joseph on meeting him, 'How is the chimney conductor programme progressing?' And then they would laugh with him and assure him that he was surely right about chimneys, but it was hard to get the custom going and put into practice.

It was at the conferences of the province of Natal that the Polygonian Democratic Front leaders used to meet. They gathered in an old farmhouse which had been abandoned by a colonist and so was used by the local boss man of that farm known to be friendly to the cause.

Those gathered together discussed their progress in terms of numbers and their advances in teaching with the promise of a new and a better world for everyone. The most difficult problems seemed easy to solve, mostly because their complexities went unrecognised. A good deal of almost romantic enthusiasm flowed through the veins of these hopeful leaders. Their defects were like the shortcomings of all select circles: a deep-rooted contempt of others; an assurance of being always right; and a conviction that no one else had attained the ultimate truth.

Army Duties

The national South African army continued its border patrols and control for reasons of security for the whole country. There were occasional incursions across the border by Marxist-style freedom fighters who hoped to draw the local population into mass insurrections, though the locals were more interested in their own local affairs, so that the incursions were little more than annoying interferences.

The army leaders used to say, 'If we can't keep our enemy outside the country, how can we keep our country safe?'

The army also made many incursions several kilometres into foreign lands to halt enemy activities at their own base camps. These attacks were justified on the grounds that the base camps were so near the border that their sole purpose must have been an invasion of South African territory when the time for this was considered suitable. The army was suitably equipped to meet any emergencies except atomic bombs which, thank God, no one in the countries around ever thought of using, nor even could. The real big dangers were landmines, sown around like seeds in a cornfield, except that the cornfields were borders hundreds of kilometres long and several kilometres wide on each side; and these mines were just as likely to be laid by other countries for their protection.

The national police were likewise engaged in civic security against criminal activity, black and white, and in the ever-constant need for motor traffic control together with the prevention of traffic in drugs. The road fatalities in the ratio of vehicles to population were the highest in the world, the high rate resulting from drunken driving, drunken walking, drunken thinking, careless driving, faulty conduct and false driving licences, as well as false identity documents issued on the black markets in the shebeen networks of the townships alongside the large cities of the country.

The secret police were yet another branch devoted to the security of South Africa. Their role was to investigate acts of sedition, subversion and even plans for revolutionary action and destruction. The police offered one hundred to five hundred rand for information leading to arrests and convictions of anyone guilty of the said subversion, sedition and revolutionary intentions. Most people caught were subjected first to an accusation, then a thrashing, questions, a two-day dry-out in the summer sun and then further questions. Very few were convicted. The judges were mostly neutral in their attitude to those who had been accused. Counsel for the defence found it easy to show that there had been false accusations, prejudiced opinions or that the evidence was defective.

Nevertheless, the security police of Special Branch felt sure there were incessant influences and activities among the working and peasant classes and the intelligentsia to build up a system for change, and change surely meant reduced security.

The communist parties the world over used to swear total allegiance to the Soviet Union, although the SA Communist Party started only in 1922, soon after those started in the European countries and had been banned as a security risk since 1949. But it was known that people from South Africa belonged to the party overseas, with its centres at Dar-es-Salaam, London, New York and Toronto. Eager speakers at school debates, mass meetings or farm workers' unions would often disappear. Further enquiries usually revealed that such eager speakers had gone abroad to find employment, most often in textile factories; possibly because the know-how for textiles could be used with advantage back in their country of Polygonia, as they sometimes called it, if they ever returned.

One such person held for questioning was Joseph Khuzwayo. He was arrested under the charge of subversion, the evidence being that he held meetings where they talked about 'working for their country'.

Joseph was given two minutes' warning by a boy runner who carried a note in hand with the words, 'The store to be searched'. Joseph was able to destroy the note and tear up the black book with branch names and meeting records in a minute, putting all the shredded pieces into three different bins together with all the rubbish he could find, distributed in such a way that reassembling the shredded pieces would be really impossible.

The secret police found nothing else incriminating because there was nothing else incriminating to find. Two sacks of potatoes were emptied onto the floor, the maize flour sacks were emptied onto the other sacks, boxes of vegetables, cool drinks, match boxes, cigarettes, clothes were all searched, as were roof spaces, drainage areas, floor spaces and paraffin tins. The most they found were Joseph's belt behind the paraffin stove, lost several months before, and Ntombifuthi's stitching scissors under the clothes pile, which showed that the secret police do have their uses after all. Joseph thanked them sincerely for cleaning out the place; but that did not stop him from being arrested. They accused him of holding regular meetings. He agreed they had had meetings in his store from 7 a.m. until 6 p.m., when people came to buy and met as they bought every day, with rather shorter hours on Sundays.

He was accused of subversive activity with hidden intentions of revolutionary change. He replied that his work was commercial with no qualities of subversion. He was accused of insulting and scornful behaviour. He replied that irony was not like sarcasm and that irony was a regular part of everyday speech. He was given the two days' dry-out during December's hot season, just before Christmas and promised help and comfort if he would name people whom he helped or who helped him to organise change through violence or subversion. He informed them that all who sold to him and bought from him helped him and his family and the village in general by patronising in his commercial enterprise, with no intentional subversion or violence.

He was tied up to a vertical pole, stripped to the waist and given twenty lashes on the back and loins; these caused large and very painful weals which bled profusely, the blood providing a feast for all the flies from miles around as it dried. There he stayed stripped to the waist for two days and one night, exposed to the glare of the sun in the day and shivering with cold at night. They had to let him go because there was no evidence for their accusations. He was released after two glasses of water and the warning that any concrete evidence of misconduct, sedition or subversion would land him in prison or worse. He was also fined a thousand rand for selling alcoholic drinks without a licence.

He left saying he would stick to commerce as he had before and he hoped they could maintain security in his area since he had suffered three break-ins costing thousands of rand.

He promised that he would obtain a licence for alcoholic drinks. He knew, however, that such a licence was impossible to procure because it required a solid building, toilets for men and women, since many people drank at the store area while talking in groups, plus the securing of the place against drunken behaviour, all of which were impossible to obtain at the time.

On his return, he assured his audience how marvellous a cold drink of water tasted, how horrible the Special Branch had been, how they had been unable to convict him of subversion because there had been none and how they had no evidence of sedition or any kind of revolutionary intentions because there had been none to find. To cement the welcome that those around him gave him on his return to the store, he gave each one present a cold drink of their choice free of charge and told them how touched he was by their concern and how he knew he could rely on their continued goodwill. His experience was identical to that of hundreds, maybe thousands throughout the country.

The Democratic Development Council of Polygonia decided soon after, around 1982, to take matters into their own hands. Passive resistance was getting nowhere and there was a need for stronger measures. The Council issued a statement saying that it believed that the use of force was justified because of the successful results that would surely follow.

This decision was circulated among the widespread cells throughout the country; each leader was to be prepared for some kind of violence. Too many innocent civilians were being subjected to unpleasant tortures or, if they were lucky, to persistent harassment with no chance of redress. Very few accused were ever found guilty of subversion and revolutionary intentions; usually only those in possession of incriminating literature such as *Rebellion and Revolution* by Nikolai Lenin, otherwise known as Vladimir Ilyich Ulianov of Soviet Russian fame, and the more recent *Quotations of President Mao Tse Tung*, the little red book published in Peking in 1972. Too many deaths were occurring in prison and were publicly attributed to suicide when it was more likely to be from gross bodily harm.

It was considered by the leaders that to stay as passive resisters to the established authorities would be cowardly and useless. How force should be applied was being seriously considered by leaders of the People's Polygonian Democracy and their advisers.

General van Wyk

The head of the police force in charge of both the civil and the secret police of the eastern province of Natal was a man of iron resolution; the iron being the strength of his determination; the resolution being the firm conviction that the status quo should remain in South Africa so that white settlers and white immigrants should remain in power. The many black workers, servants and peasants were to remain as such in the system until he was gone and buried and possibly after that.

General van Wyk, for that was his name, was committed to ensuring that the different forces under his command benefited from clear decisions at the top and were formed into cohesive units working closely with each other. Inspection of the various units was a daily task for him and the decisions were made in his office on the top fourteenth floor of Falcon House, the police headquarters. He was respected by officers and men as a straight-thinking, honest and devoted chief of this province. There was never any need to contradict him; disagreement would only lead to discussion where he was always shown to be right, although he never admitted this to others. He simply let others see for themselves that this was so.

From this position of strength people felt that there was national security, both assured and reliable; nothing could go wrong. After all, most of the thinking of those in command was supported by quotations from the bible, examples from history and the experience of peoples in their own country as well as those around.

How well had independence gone in those countries to the north, in Kenya, Nigeria, Uganda, Zaire, or in Zambia and Zimbabwe? Were people better off there since their independence? The examples of partial genocide in Uganda, Nigeria or the Congo, were they to be expected in South Africa? It was noticeable that it was the black peoples who suffered the most when white politicians were succeeded by black politicians.

If the blacks were to be safe, it was the onus of the white bosses to provide it. If the whites were to be safe, they had to provide it themselves. In the words of the famous adventurer, missionary and philanthropist, David Livingstone, 'The black man is the white man's burden.' They were as true now as when they were first stated over a century before.

So General van Wyk was conscious of his role in maintaining the strength of his security force; he was the kingpin and cornerstone of this politico-martial architecture.

While his well-organised system continued in apparent security, there was one fault and crack in van Wyk's life. He no longer loved his wife and she did not like him much either. It was not that they held different views on political or national security or many other affairs. It was simply that Marita van Wyk found the general uncaring and unlovable. He found her tedious to listen to, uninteresting and no longer companionable. She found him rather hard, with a tendency to boast and a sort of pride that she found alienated her from him. She felt as if she were no longer needed. He found any kind of sincere sympathy for the hungry, the poor and the unfortunate blacks an affront to his security system, as if it was that system which was responsible for the unfortunate conditions of the underprivileged. His lack of sympathy for their children also annoyed Marita.

The van Wyk couple had lived with each other like this for several years now; they were fixed in their duties and firm in their commitments; the sentiments of happiness and love had taken on only a secondary importance.

Their eldest son, Kobus, was constantly failing his exams in economics and accountancy at Johannesburg University, because he went out philandering excessively with young women, boozing and dancing. The second child, Marilene, would melt into tears over her many duties with her BA studies. The English studies were rather better, but still there was an awful lot of reading to get through, and her father's admonitions to be firm, to pull her socks up and to be courageous was no comfort to her at all. She struggled through the second year into the third year when she would much rather have had a husband who loved her and an infant at the breast whom she could love in return.

Essays and assignments on French writers like Rabelais, Ronsard, Racine, Rousseau and Rimbaud, she found difficult to understand and even more difficult to appreciate. She considered that the first two really belonged to the Middle Ages, with their old-fashioned ideas on living and adventure. Racine was truly of the Renaissance period, while Rimbaud tended to be mostly a dream writer of the modern age when dreams were impractical. As for Rousseau, his writings were simply unreal. His famous adage, 'Man is born free, but everywhere is in chains,' was simply ridiculous.

Marilene had been round the local hospitals with her mum during goodwill visits on Family Day, otherwise known as Easter Monday. She had been struck by the utter helplessness of newborn infants. Some were so deformed as to be quite pitiful; one with a harelip that needed a special feeding bottle, one with its guts hanging through the umbilical area where there should have been a normal umbilical scarring, a condition that could be repaired only when the child was strong enough for surgery. Another still had a large brain opening with no bone covering, and would surely die fairly soon. Once born, all children needed a decent wash to get that nasty sticky waxy stuff off their body and all needed constant feeding and toilet care to enable them to suck, suck and sleep during their first three months of life. That applied to all newborn infants, whether deformed or well formed, and it was marvellous how many newborns were in fact quite complete in their anatomy and physique, considering how very complex the little creatures were. But to say they were free seemed quite incongruous. Marilene considered the reverse of Rousseau's motto to be more true, that is, 'All are born in chains through the care that all newborns require, and later some may become free by their own endeavours, free from utter dependence on others.'

She used to complain to her mother of the tedious and unreal qualities of her studies, and most of all of the third-year French studies. Her mother tried to console her. This perhaps was the easiest of third year-studies; it was educational, giving a knowl-edge of other worlds, other writers and several different views, even if they were apparently incongruous. With effort and persistence, she would get herself a BA degree, which would enable her to follow a career, even if only part-time, with a library, a newspaper, as a schoolteacher or simply as a receptionist. It was so important to be qualified nowadays when so many women became divorcees because of rough, uncaring selfish men who sought a divorce as and when they found another woman for themselves with more appeal and excitement than the first wife.

So Marilene made the effort, passed the two majors and the other third-year subjects, obtained her BA degree and managed soon after to become engaged to a well-intentioned lawyer with whom she had four children and to whom she was to teach the excesses of Gargantua, the tragedies of Racine in the tradition of Sophocles and the utter inventions of Rousseau whose writings may have spurred on the French Revolution of 1789, but did very little to improve the lot of those who thought they had been born free but found themselves in chains.

The third child, Johannes, was a great success on the rugby field, captain of the cricket team, a great athlete, but if he passed matric, it would be some kind of scholastic miracle. His career was clearly marked out. Once matric was passed, two years with the military, then a lifetime in the police force.

This was the family, typical of many families, but it was not that happy for the head and mainstay of this community and of this country.

Robbery and Murder

General van Wyk was rarely called out to the city of Johannesburg to check on charges of theft, house-breaking and grievous bodily harm, but there was one example that aroused his interest.

It was reported that a family named Wilkinson had been attacked fifty kilometres from the city. Mr Wilkinson and his parents had been killed; Mrs Wilkinson and her three children had been beaten up, but left alive; some horses had been stolen; the house was ransacked for arms and clothing, but jewellery was not touched.

What intrigued General van Wyk was the partial extent of the crime. Why four people left alive who could give evidence; why so much material left behind during the night in question, a Friday night as it happened? The first time, he went out with two commanders of police and two patrol officers. He was looking very smart in a full blue uniform with gold buttons and gold braid plus two rows of campaign ribbons to commemorate the campaigns of North Africa, Italy and Korea, as well as the internal campaigns of Sharpville and Bonteheuval, the Rhodesian border war and the Angolan border war, campaigns in which he had taken part, all in bright colours like different sections of a rainbow.

At the place of the crime, the patrol officers found several tyre marks on gravel and lawn and broken strings. The police officers questioned the gardeners, Lovemore and Sixpence, who were both terrified out of their wits and hardly spoke, neither in Sotho, Zulu English nor in Afrikaans. The general talked to Mrs Wilkinson, whose first name was Marie. She said very little between sobs that shook her all over, apart from expletives like, 'Die bliksem kaffirs, die vuil swartes...' The general came to understand that Marie had returned from a ballet demonstration done by her seven-year-old daughter, Miriam, which her two brothers had also attended. They arrived to find the gang of four dragging the grandparents into the bushes, and taking their leave immediately with the two cars piled with hunting guns and clothes, blankets and shoes while another four were far away in the bottom field leading off four horses, two geldings, a mare and a stallion. The eldest of Marie's sons, André, had raced to his own room, set aside from the house and started firing with his .22 rifle. The gang made off post haste with their loot and a few wounds on the arms and legs. André attended his dying father under the bushes. He was bleeding profusely from chest and back wounds, and his last words were, 'Justice must be done, my son.'

In fact, the three children and their mother had not been hurt, contrary to the report, but were suffering from shock and overwhelming grief. Marie Wilkinson, née Marais, grieved for months for the loss of her husband and parents, kept to the house, wouldn't answer telephone calls, never went out and refused all invitations, occupying herself only with the children's meals and clothes. Her feelings swung between anger and thoughts of revenge, and self-pity and pondering about the value of living in such unhappy circumstances. The local dominee was a great help, coming to visit her at least weekly, usually before his Sunday services, which she eventually attended.

General J van Wyk also liked to visit sometimes, telling her news about progress in the criminal investigation. Two robbers were identified by the housemaid through a one-way mirror at the police station. They admitted nothing more than having stolen for gain. Two horse thieves were caught without any horses through boasting of their escapade in the local township; they were betrayed by eavesdroppers who held a grudge against them because of substantial unpaid debts. The horse thieves thought the horses were to be sold to horse breeders somewhere north of Cape Town.

Marie slowly recovered from her grief and used to look forward to van Wyk's visits, when he would talk of his plan for a secure and safe South Africa, plans that included more informers among the working-class black population, who were rewarded for their services. Likewise, he envisaged an increased cooperation among the different defence forces so that information could and would be more promptly shared, enabling the police to know quickly of any civil intransigence the army might discover and vice versa.

After six months of such visits van Wyk would kiss Marie goodbye affectionately on leaving her. The general admired her strength and her resolution to continue for the sake of the children and for her country. He was glad to share his emotional and intellectual feelings and opinions with someone so sympathetic. After a year of this friendship, their mutual affections became more than handshakes and kisses.

The children also suffered grief and despondency, but went on with their studies and sport as was expected during their school hours. It was only much later they expressed their resentments towards horse murderers and thieves when confiding to their close friends. That was much later on, when they were able to express their ideas and sentiments without the crushing sense of grief blocking up their other feelings.

The Intelligence Service

The South African Intelligence Service was a part of the Special Branch and a division of the civil police. Its task was to maintain peace and protect citizens and their property from those with no property who tried to acquire other people's through guile and deceit. The service devoted its time to solving crimes, seeking out drug traders and preventing drug traffic at the many borders of the country. More than this, the service maintained security against sedition and sought out any activity that could lead to insurrections.

Marius Wessels was head of Intelligence. After ten years with the service, starting as a lieutenant of the police force, for just a year, he had opted for work with Intelligence because of his education, international studies and because he believed in his country and he thought this was the best way to serve it. His biggest interest was the maintenance of trust and cooperation between all peoples, blacks, coloureds, Asiatics and whites as well as cooperation among the police, defence or other government ministries of all groups, as far as possible, with their many different functions. All these peoples were part of his country, South Africa. He used to say his country belonged to everyone who lived in it. He used to say that his country had been built up from a savage wild place into a civilised, organised place with good roads, modern medicine, a decent education system for most people, modern agriculture, a large manufacturing base internationally acclaimed through the efforts of the many ancestors who had come to live and work here over the last three hundred years. All these Europeans from Holland, Germany, France or England, it was these people who had built up the country into a thriving profitable place, fit for any who chose to immigrate and live here, and a loss to any who chose to emigrate.

Marius's second-in-command, Jacob du Preez, generally agreed with his chief's beliefs, but differed in insisting that all criminals needed both a corrective and a penalty for their crimes. He scorned the excusing of criminals with extenuating circumstances, like drunkenness or some psychological distortion, which he considered most times to be blown out of all proportion to their influences. Marius went along with this strict discipline up to a point, but said that decency in all things was the prime factor. 'Even the hardened criminal must be treated with decency and be made to realise that to be decent is better than to be violent and abusive', he used to proclaim.

His theories went further than this. His big theory was that organised socialism was a curse and the source of more damage than any other philosophy in the world during this century. As an example, he stated that the National Socialism of Germany had been a great influence in that country to provide the working class with better wages, good working conditions, arranged medical aid and precautions for safer conditions plus pension schemes; right, that was fine. But once National Socialism had become an international power, it had gone on to ruin Europe for close on ten years. Likewise the Soviet socialists might have benefited their workers, though he doubted it, when he thought of the fate of the kulaks as an example, but as an international force, it had become a complete menace.

The fact is that socialism had given a whole new meaning to people's lives, where before there had not been much meaning, and this applied to the intellectual as well as to the man in the street!

Marius maintained that you cannot get a meaningful life through political theory. He said that one gets a meaning and an understanding through metaphysics, a philosophy or spiritual guidance. 'You can't cut through a log by using a hammer,' was one of his sayings. Witness the exploitation of poor peoples all over the world, encouraged, taught and led on to spread violence and revolution aided with arms and ammunition. The communist promise was intended to stir dissension, aggression, then violence, aided by a programme for progress which would allow the leaders of this new group to be in charge in place of the previous leaders whom they had always accused of inefficiency, degeneration and incompetence. So it was in many hundreds of places in the world.

And how much benefit had the new revolutionaries bestowed on those they had promised to help? Marius believed that the benefits bestowed went only to those who had become the new leaders; all those other proletarian workers were no better off and in most cases were considerably worse off than before. Not only was Soviet aid going to revolutionary armies, but many weapons were landing up with criminal organisations whose only interests were robbery and the settling of vendettas of several generations standing. Hence Marius's solemn adage, 'In this century, socialism has ruined the world!' With all this theory and theorising, Jacob du Preez used to say that there can be no absolute justice; instead justice is set in relation to the needs and rules of a country fixed in a certain place and time, as shown in history. Marius countered that there was no firm definition of justice, but there was a description that deserved a mention. He affirmed, 'Justice is that which is to be found just by a just man.' Jacob riposted that such a statement begged the question about justice. It gave no details or indications of how justice was established except by referring to a just man's judgement; once in a while, he could very easily fail in determining justice.

Marius answered that justice is not a quality or a quantity like a mathematical equation or a calculation in physics. This was why an all-round education was so important to give an overall picture and understanding to the law-makers. Likewise, Marius used to add that other qualities used often in human assessments were also impossible to define, though they could be described. He mentioned the concepts of truth, goodness and beauty; these qualities are frequently referred to in normal conversation and descriptions. But could Jacob define them?

Despite all this talk, Marius was aware that action and knowledge were the constant necessities of security. He was aware now that many black workers were more truculent and more self-possessed than before, with reports coming in of mass meetings together with insolence from many different workplaces. He wanted to know what was being discussed, but never obtained a clear explanation nor explicit statements of subjects discussed. All he was told was that the workers were encouraged to work together. 'We must be united,' was the motto that was repeatedly reported to him.

This remark did not satisfy Marius Wessels at all. He said, 'What is this "We must be united" business? I want some sort of explanation and insight into any anti-government activity. Is this all you people on the lookout for dangerous influences can tell me?' He suggested more energetic methods of getting information. 'You don't have to be brutal about it; you can use sinister methods without being cruel, thoroughly vicious and really nasty.'

So inquisitions continued against all sorts of suspects, usually heads of worker gangs and those who were obvious leaders in stating resentment or disagreements about work systems or the injustice of salaries with regard to ethnic groups. Unfortunately, the officers of the security system often took it on themselves to take harsh measures, which sometimes resulted in prison deaths, in the hope that some worthwhile confession might result to justify the unpleasant ways that were being used. And that was not only inside the country.

The security threat had in fact involved members checking potential revolutionaries as far away as in Great Britain and the Americas. There were reports of parcel bombs going off in people's faces and blasting off hands in these far-off places. Who was responsible was left to the imagination.

When these incidents of gross bodily harm were reported to Marius, he was visibly worried. This kind of cloak-and-dagger stuff could not go on! It must either break out in open conflict or there must be some resolution and mutual agreement on all sides in place of conflict.

The Lobola

It was time for Joseph to pay the bride price called the *lobola* in Southern Africa. Only by paying the *lobola* could Joseph claim Nonhlanhla as his wife. She lived in a suburb of Durban called Kwabushu with her mother, Agnes Dlamini, and Grandma, Jabulile Hadebe. Agnes's husband had been killed during a faction fight some years before, involving arguments over the rights of property concerning the use of two acres of land that everyone used anyway, together with other complaints nurtured into a cause for conflict between the Dlamini and the Gumede tribes. That had been the end of Daddy Dlamini for this family of females.

Mother Agnes and her daughters – there were two others – had eked out a living through housekeeping and laundry work for moneyed people. Now the little fellow was four years old and at last his father had made contact. The little fellow, Nimrod, had started asking about where his father was. Other children had their fathers at home in the evenings. When was his father coming home? His mother would tell him that Daddy was working for them on the gold mines at Johannesburg; that was the usual excuse given for absent fathers, and he should be coming home soon.

It took Joseph Khuzwayo six months to contact her through the principal director of Democratic Affairs in Johannesburg. The delay was due to the fact that there was poor liaison between the Johannesburg and the Natal principals; each request tended to be put aside to be considered later. When Joseph had her address, he wrote to say how glad he was to know where she was and how was she? How was the boy? And that he wished to pay the bride price or the *lobola*.

Her relatives were delighted to hear this news. Maybe they could stop worrying about living on the breadline and start living with some comfort and luxuries at last. Joseph had mentioned that he was a poor proletarian with the earnings of a small food and general store at Esigodeni in the province of Natal where he had to care for his mother, a younger sister and two employees, plus pay the *induna* rates on his store and on the land attached.

After due consideration among her elders, it was agreed that Nonhlanhla was valued at ten cows plus two bulls together with ten thousand rand but, because of his poor background and bearing in mind the decency of socialist camaraderie, they agreed to four cows, one bull and five thousand rand. When could they expect the price? they asked. His answer was prompt: in six months' time.

In the meantime, he was able to visit them near Durban and was delighted to see his prospective wife still looking young, beautiful and active. He hugged his little son, Nimrod, fervently and with genuine affection, leaving him a toy train with a coach and trailer, chosen after careful advice from friends: a rattle and balloons was for smaller children, a tricycle for older children.

Joseph left after two nights and two days with the family, leaving behind a wailing son and a sad fiancée, with the words, 'We will make progress together.'

Joseph went to see the nearest cattle farm, twenty kilometres from Kwabushu. There he met a Mr Ernie Oosthuiysen with whom he talked of cow and bull prices. They agreed on a thousand rand for each cow and fifteen hundred for a bull, to be delivered by cattle truck once the total sum was paid. This was all arranged within the six months. Suddenly his prospective in-laws had their five beasts delivered to the house, a pondoki of dried mud walls with a thatched roof and no chimney! They were prepared, however. One cow was tethered to a pole nearby, the rest were herded by two cattle boys into a cattle kraal ten kilometres away, costing ten rand per beast per month.

One cow was disposed of with a couple of sledgehammer blows to the head, rendering it unconscious and two deep stab wounds on each side of the neck. The animal was skinned; the carcass was disembowelled, slung up on a horizontal pole, fixed between two trees, cleaned out of all viscera and the meat left to mature with two strong boys on guard to stop thieving. Two days later, all of their relatives and friends, the Dlaminis and the

Hadebes, were called and gathered to celebrate the wedding ceremony of the bride. This was a celebration of the bride's family only. Joseph had left a lump sum of five hundred rand, part of the *lobola*. With this, maize flour was boiled to make a porridge called *putu* in the south and sadza in the north. Further, there was relish: three buckets of spinach, onions, and tomatoes boiled and mixed to go with the roast meat and the maize porridge. But most important was the *Amahewu*, also called *Amajuba*; this was litres of milk fermented with maize flour for two days that served both as a drink and a food, plus the fermented distilled drink *tshwala* for the hard drinkers.

Discussions, speeches and dancing went on into the night with swinging, rolling, rocking movements to the sounds of drums, marimbas and flutes. The two hundred and ten people were satiated and happy at this marriage feast, excepting for four people who had fights over claims to property that were intensified by insults about their physiognomy. One had a nose that was too big, another's ears were distorted, another had a scarred-up left eye, while the fourth had an ungainly flat head. Their quarrels led to stab wounds with assegais; the one-eyed and the odd-ears men were killed from chest wounds. The other two men melted away into the dark alleys of the township to avoid further conflict with the victims' friends. Apart from this fracas, it was a pleasurable and much enjoyed evening.

A week later, Nonhlanhla and her son Nimrod left Kwabushu to join Joseph Khuzwayo at Esigodeni. Enough of the bride price had been paid to allow Nonhlanhla to join up with her future legal husband.

Nonhlanhla was shown all around as was normal; she met the people of the store and the village, so that in a short time she was quite at home and glad to take part in all the necessary jobs a sensible woman can be expected to do. In fact, she served as shopkeeper, housekeeper, mother and wife. From then on, she was his property but by virtue of his further education by the Democratic People's Programme for Progress in Tanzania, he respected her person as an important part of his property, and soon she was expecting again; in her second pregnancy, she delivered a sister, Buhle, for Nimrod.

Joseph was able to pay off about five hundred rand a month to his mother-in-law and so paid off the remainder of the *lobola* over the next year. Now she really was his wife, and he was able to celebrate his completed wedding with a roast cow at his Esigodeni home together with the *putu*, the vegetable relish, *Amajuba*, local wine of the country and even tshwala, brandy, gin and vodka, very like the party of a year ago, but now with his own mother, and his mother-in-law, gogo Dlamini, who came all the way from Kwabushu. The older woman, gogo Hadebe, still alive, could not face the ten-hour journey and preferred to stay at her home with her two dogs and a cat.

She was happy to stay in her wattle hut of thick thatching with her memories of eighty-four years; in those far-off times there were far fewer white people and also less blacks, though the Indian population was growing by immigration, brought in to cut and stack the sugar cane.

The thrash that Joseph put on to celebrate his final wedding contract was reinforced by the well-known and respected Fr Burley after a series of instructions intended to seal the allegiance of these two already married people to church duties for the rest of their lives. They were taught how fulfilling and rewarding a happy marriage would be. At least they knew that their union was already fruitful. To Joseph it seemed that Fr Burley was bringing God to the people by his instruction and his services. Joseph was interested in bringing the poor working-class proletariat and the peasants up to a worthwhile living standard. He and his own kind thought that once that had been achieved, God's plan for the people, whatever it was, could then be considered seriously. He thought the former programme was a luxury whereas the latter was a communal necessity. What he would actually do once he met up with God's plan, he was not sure.

For all their differences, Joseph always felt a respect for the now ageing venerable Fr Burley. He it was who had set Joseph on the path to appreciate the value of learning and of knowledge with his interesting sermons twice a month at the little village of Esigodeni that he had listened to many years before.

Van Wyk's Gardener

Members of the Democratic People's Party of Polygonia were told to watch out always for ways of reducing the power, influence, unity or reputation of those in command. Polygonia was the name given to the eastern province of Natal and the area around the Kruger Park by these members of the Democratic Party. They used to say, 'If we chip away at the block of power, eventually the whole structure will come falling down; but we must do it with the minimum of crime or advertisement.' That was the instruction which went out to all groups such as Joseph Khuzwayo's Tuesday evening monthly meetings and he was able to talk about this with embellishments to illustrate the point. He used an example from *A Tale of Two Cities*, thus, 'Clouds may take weeks and months to build up, but once they are thick and strong enough, then the thunder and lightning comes down in a matter of seconds to strike down standing structures. So it is with our organisation; we must wait until the moment is right for striking.'

General Johannes van Wyk's gardener was one who was able to contribute information to the group to which he belonged. Jabulani, shortened to Jabu, was a man of little education. He had passed standard three at a school which taught him to write, read and make simple calculations. This enabled him to cut the lawns and the hedges; clean the car; plant roses, chrysanthemums or nasturtiums in the front garden and carrots, cabbages, peas, beans and lettuce in the back garden. His qualities as a gardener to the general were reliability, obedience and politeness. He came to work every morning at seven o'clock without the effects of a hangover on a Monday morning, unlike many of his comrades. He would continue until four o'clock in the afternoon, with an hour's break for lunch, and then it was agreed he could knock off, unless there was urgent work to do, as once when they had to put out a fire in the tool shed, started by one of the children. At another time, it was chasing away locusts by banging dustbin lids together to frighten them off. That had happened in the early fifties before the locust menace had been stamped out with aerial spraying. Once there had been an invasion of goats which were being herded to the animal market on a Saturday morning. Someone had left the garden gate open and suddenly thirty goats were seen invading the place at the early hour of five o'clock in the morning. They had eaten up most of the flowers and half the vegetables, and were chased away with great agitation and annoyance by everyone in the house and garden, adults and children, including the general's two young ones, who found it most amusing.

Jabulani lived in the small servants' quarters at the back of the garden with his wife and his three children in two rooms, plus a toilet and shower outside. He was glad of his post and lodging. His wife also worked in the house, doing cleaning, laundry and ironing, but not cooking. Muhle had never learned the art of Western cooking. All she could do was roast meat over a fire and boil maize flour to make *putu* and boil relish vegetables of all kinds to go with the *putu*. She never learned to bake, fry nor oven roast, and did not much want to learn either.

Jabulani was contented with his lot, but he would have liked more possessions. He had started work at this house and garden forty years before as a gardener and forty years later he was still the gardener. He had risen from being assistant gardener to chief gardener at a place where there were only two gardeners. He thought that if he had joined the shoe factory down the road from the beginning, he might have done better; after thirty years he would have been boss of the works team. At the clothes factory farther away, after thirty years he would not have been making clothes but selling them at the many outlets that the factory used, altogether more interesting than this garden or the workbench all day long.

But his wife consoled him with the thought that such work meant living in a man's hostel nearby and she would have been living and confined to a tribal trust land fifty kilometres away in the area called Komdoni. There he would have had to pay five hundred rand to get permission from the tribal chief to build a hut with a circular wall and thatching and two small doors for herself, together with the use of land around, enough for a vegetable patch ten metres square with some chickens to go with it for a monthly rent of ten rand. Perhaps she would have been a casual labourer helping at the local store when someone was sick or hoeing the maize fields at the farms ten kilometres away during the growing season of January, February and March. Muhle told Jabu that their position would have been very different, with him seeing the family, children and friends once every two weeks: what a difference from what they had now. Secretly, she knew that if Jabulani had taken a post with the shoe or clothes factory, once he had had a room to himself, as happened to assistant boss men of the factories, he would have acquired a second live-in wife from a cheap shebeen in the area, someone who did not need the payment of a *lobola*. This had already been paid by another man who could have dismissed her for any number of reasons, like infertility, or who may have died so that she was widowed and penniless.

Muhle used to tell her husband and children how happy and fortunate they were to have their jobs and their small two-room quarters. It was true that the water was always cold, but they had to accept that. Most months the cold water was a relief in the hot weather. It was only in July, August and September that water had to be boiled up to supplement the cold water and so make body washing bearable.

All the same, Jabu used to look at the large spacious colourful house of the general and his family and he wished he could have such a fine house. In fact, after forty years of working around the place, replacing broken glass, fixing new awnings, repairing fences and gates, painting and planting, he felt the house and home was partially his. He came to believe that the house was his after forty years of devoted service and care. Then, when and if ever he had the chance to own it, what a difference he would make to the house and to himself. He would fill each room with a family unit, instead of there being only five people living in this grand big house, with its occasional visitors; aunts, uncles, cousins, grandparents and friends, he would let into it up to ten family groups, charging each group fifty rand a month.

There would be one family group in each of the bedrooms,

that would be four of them, two in the lounge, one by the television corner, another by the sofa and fireplace where the Labradors usually lay about, six; two family groups would fit easily in the dining room, sharing the chairs, of course, eight; then one unit around the kitchen area; another by the bathroom area, again sharing the use of toilet and bath; and finally his old servants' quarters outside, making eleven family groups in all. He would be well off with all this rental coming in. His own family could fit nicely in the top room or attic.

My goodness, he thought to himself, I would make for myself a worthwhile profit, instead of having to cut and dig around the garden for five and a half days every week as I have done for the last forty years, starting at ten rand a week, now receiving a hundred rand weekly, with some rations and handouts.

He went on brooding like this until he really did believe that the house might belong to him in a special new-order sort of way. Perhaps if all the whites did leave this country, and many were leaving or had left over the last five years, then perhaps he could claim the house as his own by virtue of occupation and usage, an example of possession by appropriation, he thought.

In fact, there is an understanding in law circles that possession can be claimed through many years' usage as if one were in possession if it can be shown that over many years there was this usage. The conditions were expressed as 'Nec vi, nec clam, nec precario', that is, neither by force, nor stealth nor with permission, extending over thirty and a third years, or in some places just thirty years, though naturally this aspect of law was unknown to Jabulani. Perhaps by some legal agreement, Jabulani might just get his wish of possession, though it would surely be unlikely since there were so many with stronger claims to this property, such as all the near relatives.

It was while he was pondering like this one afternoon that he remembered there was a meeting within the hour with the Democratic People's Party for Progress down at the shoe factory where workers finished the day with two mugs of *Amahewu* Zulu beer and then started their party talks. Once there and after the preliminaries were over, he was asked if he had anything of interest to tell them. He told them that he had clearly noticed his boss, General van Wyk, was absenting himself three nights a week because the car was not in the garage until it returned at about five or six o'clock in the morning, and usually during the nights of Monday, Wednesday and Friday. He admitted he did not know why the general was away, nor what his wife thought or knew of it, but he did know that this had become a regular practice of the general's. Jabulani did not think this was of much significance, but since there were no obvious police or army actions going on, it did seem strange that there was such a regular absence on the general's part. Jabu thought he ought to say something to the group of fifteen people assembled at the meeting instead of staying silent and dumb as was usually the case. After all, if someone as important as the general was away so often during this peace time period, there must be something going on that was being kept secret from the public. The leader of the group took note of this fact and agreed this was something that might deserve checking on. Was this the result of some international plot that was being arranged, perhaps with the United States of America, or was it some personal adventure the general had got himself involved in?

So the political meeting broke up and Jabu thought no more about it. Little did he know that this piece of information would come to change the lives of many people in South Africa.

Renamo and Frelimo

Once it was known that the general was away three days weekly from home, his absence was checked at police headquarters by Eric Mthethwa, also a member of the Polygonian Democratic Party. He worked at the garage section of the police headquarters and was able to confirm that the general did not stay at headquarters all day long, but left his post pretty regularly at 3.30 p.m., sometimes with other officers, presumably commanders, for meetings. It was easy for observers to spot where the general was going and check either at his home in the northern suburbs or sometimes at a farm eastwards where criminals had raided and killed six months before; at the home in fact of Marie Wilkinson, née Marais, with her three children. That was now an established fact, to be remembered and catalogued by those who wanted to take part in chicanery.

In the meantime there were invitations from Portuguese East Africa for collusion between their Democratic People's Party and the South African one. The leaders of the two organisations argued that cooperation between their two countries was highly desirable. PEA, now known as Mozambique, had overthrown their colonial masters in 1975, but there was still strong disagreement and big differences of opinion among the new leaders. Some wished for the development of international socialism with faithful adherence to Marxist–Leninism. Others preferred their socialism to be directed towards local and national interests. The latter were the Renamo which can be understood to mean 'The Regime for a National and a Military Organisation'. It was too soon, they argued, for international involvement, so they strongly disagreed with 'The Freeing Liberation of Marxist Organisations', which can be understood to mean the political party known as Frelimo. Frelimo had the support of international socialism backed by the Soviets, and hence they were much stronger that their Renamo partners backed only by national interests with private enterprise connections. In fact, they developed not as partners, but as contesting powers. They had both developed in opposition to established Portuguese colonial rule with its three hundred years of history. Both partners defamed and maligned their old colonial leaders with promises of freedom, self-rule and self-determination when they were rousing the populace in their large country of half a million square kilometres in extent. But after acquiring power, position and advantages in the rule of their country, the two partners had developed an animosity to each other which had become belligerent, antagonistic and finally murderous.

The cooperation suggested to the Democratic People's Republic of South Africa promised advantages to both sides. There would be greater power by virtue of combined efforts. Later there would be increased trade opportunities and better knowledge and know-how once these different forces got going together properly in a spirit of cooperation, forgetting their differences for the sake of progress that surely would be advantageous to all.

Joseph Khuzwayo was involved with consideration of this invitation to cooperation, since he was now head of the section for democracy in Natal. He met the leaders of the several provinces in a partly broken down tobacco barn quite near the Mozambique border. They talked through the night into the next morning with swarms of ideas flowing from the different people present. Joseph hit on a plan which he thought suited the circumstances.

He believed that his movement was still not strong enough to combat the military and police forces of his country, but he believed that a scheme involving his comrades, together with Frelimo in the south and Renamo in the north, might succeed. They were to unite in spite of their differences for this campaign, then they could carry out a programme of insurrection that would enable them to force some sort of capitulation.

He suggested hit-and-run tactics from the east into the eastern part of Polygonia, threatening and even overrunning military and police posts in the area. This would bring the rest of the peace-time army and all the other forces of defence into the eastern area of that threatened country. Just at the right moment, one person,

George Olivier, a member of their Democratic committee would be infiltrated to create confusion and chaos. George Olivier had been living in Rhodesia, now called Zimbabwe for many years. He had finished his Rhodesian years in the army during Mr Ian Smith's tenure and during UDI, the unilateral declaration of independence option the country had exercised against the Westminster government. George had become an officer, rising to the rank of captain and had been aide-de-camp and adjutant to the general of the Selous Scouts. He had witnessed much killing, both soldiers and civilians, which he had found distasteful and disgusting. This had caused him to turn his coat, as people say, becoming sympathetic to the blacks and scornful of white rule and attempted domination. That was when he had left to set up a fish-and-chip shop at Hout Bay near Cape Town, a peaceful life to help him forget the traumatic experiences and horror in the north. His recreation was amateur dramatics, which he much enjoyed, especially the roles of tough nasty domineering characters like Iago in *Othello* and Captain Bligh in *Mutiny on the Bounty*.

Joseph pointed out that this was just the man who could help to do the job. With a touch-up of his facial features and a change of clothing, George Olivier could look very much like the present head of police, namely General Johannes van Wyk. Many coloured men of the country looked like their European counterparts; just a suggestion of curly hair and an olive skin showed that they had had relatives of Negroid or Negro-Indian ancestry many years ago. George Olivier was just such a man. They reckoned that, at the right moment, George could take van Wyk's place and for one week he could issue orders leading to confusion and disadvantage everywhere, while the military branch of the People's Democratic Party would break out into action and attempt to master the situation. This crazy plan was accepted as worth a trial and from then on the committee sent encouraging communications to Frelimo and Renamo forces suggesting a trial of strength, not an all-out war but a probing action to see how they went against the long-established power and domination that the military and police of South Africa had maintained for so long. It was worth a try after so many years of being secondary citizens in their own country and enduring insults, hurt, and abuse illustrated by the examples of serious or grievous bodily harm leading to deaths in prison and attributed to 'prison suicides'!

Bater e Correr

First the campaign of 'Bater e Correr', or hit-and-run, as it is known in English, had to be started. Frelimo forces assembled along their western borders and met up with officers of the Polygonian freedom fighters; they conferred together in order to coordinate their plans. The Frelimo personnel were all dressed up in the dark blue uniforms of the army of that country with officers easily distinguished by a bright red five-pointed star affixed to their berets. The Polygonian officers, meanwhile, could not flaunt anything so obviously military. They were dressed to look like gardeners and road workers, carrying in their hands an old spade or a garden fork. It was agreed that the Mozambican forces would advance in a week's time, Saturday afternoon, using cars packed with infantry, ten men plus the driver in Chevrolet cars, stolen and prepared for the advance. The operation would start at three o'clock. That would give them three hours before nightfall and, with complete surprise, they hoped to go quite a few kilometres into the country before being forced to stop and defend themselves. It was further understood that once the invaders had ground to a halt, perhaps on the defensive themselves at that stage, their cars would probably be unusable. That would be the time when the Frelimo or Renamo troops, who were further north along the border, would take it upon themselves to walk back to camp. At this point, they could consider that they had completed their side of the bargain. If the cars were still in working order, well and good, but they had to avoid the awful tragedy of troops on the same side of the campaign firing and shooting at each other as the invaders returned to Maputo.

With this aspect agreed on, the Polygonians melted away back to their temporary base across the border with their own men to await their comrades the next week, after which they would be busy setting up roadblocks in order to keep the national army as preoccupied as possible.

Come the next Saturday afternoon, the Frelimo forces pushed right into South Africa without so much as a warning shot. It was the time when most normal people were enjoying sporting events and going to their local clubs and relaxing after another week's work. The military forces easily overran the Customs offices, blockhouses and other opposition on the borders. They had ridden ten to a car; two in front with the driver, four pairs at the back with the roofs off and the back seats readjusted with the pairs sitting back to back with rifles ready for any targets to shoot up in front or behind as the case might be. There was an abundance of ammunition, grenades plus landmines in the boots of the cars, all stolen vehicles. All opposition was taken completely by surprise.

By Monday morning the invading forces were three hundred kilometres into the country and setting up roadblocks with timber and boulders; the infantry infiltrated the bush and farm lands, and occupied military camps where only a quarter of the personnel were present. By Tuesday, the invaders met with the first real military opposition coming from the west; infantry in troop carriers and six-ton tanks with light machine guns.

Major Labuschagne, in charge of the national army in the region, knew well the procedures needed against an invasion, given his twenty years of military experience.

'We'll soon stop these kaffirs,' he boasted. 'How can they have any chance of success? They're just a bunch of poorly trained native warriors hoping for gain and without any back-up.'

In fact, it turned out to be the biggest conflict in his military experience. One word of the major's is now a dirty word in South Africa's vocabulary. In the last century, this K word was used in history books. One reads of the 'First Kaffir War of 1779' and the 'Seventh Kaffir War of 1847', the inevitable fights between settled farmers and nomadic tribes. Also current were Kaffirboom, a red flowering tree, now called erythrhynum; likewise 'kaffir corn'; just two examples of words now frowned upon. This was not the major's concern at the time. He was intent on resisting conquest and providing security, and he was going to have a fine experience of what it costs.

At the first roadblock, the leading tank, called a ferret, banged against branches and boulders, setting off several hand grenades primed to explode when dislodged. The two front rubber wheels were blown off, for these six-tonners ran on rubber wheels and not on tracks. As the occupants, the driver and the gunner, opened the hatch the better to look around, they were gunned down by small-arms fire from nearby concealed enemy infantry. Those behind returned fire with their light machine guns and, as others deployed through the bushlands, three had their feet blown off by landmines placed beforehand around the area of the roadblock. It was then that Major Labuschagne realised that he was up against professionals of sorts rather than amateurs. He was able to signal back to base through short-wave radio transmission to report the seriousness of the invasion, together with the request for helicopter evacuation, 'Casevac', for the two dead and three wounded soldiers.

The Casevac chopper arrived two hours later to land two kilometres down the road with infantry guarding the area in a radius of one kilometre around the spot, keeping the aircraft safe in its descent and ascent. In the meantime, infantry spread out carefully through the bush country in pursuit of an enemy who had disappeared. One dead man was found some distance from the first encounter in a dark blue shirt and shorts and nothing else. He'd been stripped of all other possessions and left for dead by his comrades from abdominal wounds impossible to treat and care for at that time and place.

Sixth Commando, for that was the name of Major Labuschagne's outfit, proceeded cautiously and pressed on another ten kilometres towards the Mozambique border, met with no further opposition and the major decided to sit out the night alongside the road, under canvas with a stream twenty metres away. The place was mine-free, having been checked by the two engineers, and the unit called up base HQ again, suggesting reinforcements for the next day so as to be able to push on to the border now only ninety kilometres away. It was then that the major learned that there were two roadblocks behind him, either of which would halt any reinforcements coming up to join him.

'That decides it,' he told his men. 'We're here for some time; don't waste ammunition and we must keep constantly in touch while spread out in this bushland as we proceed eastwards to the border.'

The next day, another two of his men were wounded as they scoured the country one kilometre from the road. Again the Casevac helicopter arrived two hours after wireless contact and call-up. This time the major asked the orderly for five bottles of spirits on his next visit, 'Just to help things along during the long evening hours!'

As it happened, the next day there were three casualties, two mine injuries to feet and bullet wounds to the chest as Sixth Commando were entering a mountain pass with narrow sides, an obvious place for an ambush. The Casevac duly arrived with news that the reinforcements were proceeding slowly because of many landmines and guerrilla-type warfare at every turn and rise of the road. Furthermore, it had to be understood that this was one of several roads leading east, all infested with freedom fighters, guerrillas or terrorists, whatever one wanted to call them.

Mike Ferguson, for that was the orderly's name, informed the major that he had been unable to obtain five bottles of spirits, but he had managed to persuade the hospital quartermaster to let him have a five-litre tin of methylated spirits, which he handed over to the major while feeling quite proud of himself. The major mumbled a grudging thanks and returned to his base tent to show his sergeant the tin.

'That's what we get for our five litres of spirits I asked for from that orderly, Mike Somebody; he must be wet behind the ears.'

For the next three days Sixth Commando advanced cautiously and reached the border post, arranged gun emplacements with overlapping arcs of fire, and sat out doing garrison duty for the ensuing few days. The commando now numbered twenty-five men and lived on roast baboon with river water for these three days. The iron food rations were finished and all brandy, whisky and beer supplies quite drained off. The medical officer, Doctor Botha, was able to help. He had brought many supplies for stitching wounds, supposedly for wounded enemy troops, but he was most helpful in supplying sedatives for the officers and NCOs in the form of Valium and Librax to supplement the cool clear river water they were forced (and lucky they were to have it) to fall back on during their last three days of garrison duty.

Finally, Colonel Billingham met up with them after his Fifth Commando had cleared four roadblocks together with road and hill ambushes for the loss of five killed and eight wounded. He announced his arrival with the words, 'The British have broken through again,' much to the annoyance of the other, mostly Afrikaner, soldiers.

Colonel Harold Billingham had started his military career at Sandhurst, having passed WOSB, the War Office Selection Board, to train soon after as a lieutenant before military operations in Malaya. He had assisted in the army's task of stopping the communists takeover there in the insurgency of the late fifties. General Sir Gerald Templer had been the High Commissioner and director of military operations. Lieutenant Billingham had learned the effective use of police and military forces working together against the insurgents in conjunction with the civilian population to free Malaya from the communist influence that was coming through from mainland China. From there he went to Kenya to combat Mau Mau with his regiment, the Northumberland Fusiliers. It was then that he developed a liking for Africa and was accepted as an officer in the Durban Light Infantry. Harold never lost his admiration for the English-speaking people, their Parliament, their history, military and civilian, and the monarchy with all the pomp and tradition. But after three years of army life abroad, he found the English climate too miserable, and so was glad to live and work in South Africa while proclaiming that British was best and that it was a crying shame that the British Empire was being reduced in size and in importance.

'We are the policemen of the world,' he used to say, 'and you will see how disorder will follow with the loss of British law and administration.'

His arrival was a great relief to Major Labuschagne. It was gratifying for the major's outfit that they had been able to carry out their orders to reach the border post and man it, as well as clear the road, even though it had taken five days with several casualties. Likewise, it was very pleasing for the major that the colonel had arrived with much needed reinforcements.

Colonel Billingham's morale was rather better than his subordinate's because he had been able to shuttle back and forth from army headquarters as his men had cleared and made the road safe. In fact, it could be said that his arrival was curative in preventing the shaking attacks, not a rare condition among long-serving service personnel.

Colonel Billingham was interested to show the major a scrap of paper they had found on a prisoner.

'We captured very few prisoners,' the colonel admitted. 'We either caught up with dead bodies, mostly stripped when we found them, or else the enemy just disappeared, always eastwards. In this way we would only catch glimpses of them through binoculars cresting hill peaks ahead of us. Our Kaspirs were not able to follow over mountain and hill areas, with dongas, ravines or rivers more than two feet deep. But we did manage to catch one fanatic who decided to run westward instead of the other way. A shot grazed his temple, knocked him out and we emptied his pockets. He escaped during the night, killing one of the guards in the process, but this paper shows clearly "Bater e Correr", that's hit-and-run in Portuguese,' said the colonel. 'Does this mean this is just a side show? I'm damned if I know what's going on, and I just hope they know back at headquarters.'

General van Wyk's Last Hours

Meanwhile, George Olivier had got himself in place as a general, pretending to be head of the police force. Taking up this post had been much easier than he and his accomplices had ever hoped. His captain's uniform and identity as Captain du Toit, acquired just a week before at a roadblock on the eastern border of the country, gave him immediate entry, and the same was true for his lieutenant, Cronje, likewise a coloured man called Japie de Villiers with an olive skin that any white man could acquire quite plausibly after a two-week holiday on the beautiful sunny shores of Mauritius.

They had been told clearly, 'Do not get entry to police head-quarters on the ground floor, for that is where you will be searched most intensely. You must gain entry into the basement parking area, where the security checks are much more lax.'

They entered the area with a stolen BMW, a fitting car for a captain of the force, and parked as near to the lift as space allowed, after a check by Tommy Mthethwa, also one of their men. From there they went up to the fourteenth floor by lift. There was another check outside the general's office at 8.30 a.m. before they entered a large office, well furnished with three armchairs, bookcases and a carpeted floor. At the writing desk of Stinkwood sat the general in his magnificence. There were preliminary greetings; Lieutenant Cronje requested directly and to the point for police reinforcements to the eastern borders, while Captain du Toit walked to the window behind the desk, admired the view, and turned around with the general distracted and attentive to Cronje. Two shots with a .22 pistol and silencer followed to the back of the head and left temple; two entry wounds with no exit wounds. The general was dead immediately. His uniform was removed and he was bundled into the cupboard. A few blood traces were wiped up and concealed, so that George Olivier became General van Wyk in a matter of ten minutes. He reckoned he had at most one week to effect diversionary influences before the police officers or the two women in his life became suspicious and suspected that the real general had disappeared.

Cronje was dispatched to the second floor by order of the new chief, who phoned the sorting office and ordered that Cronje act as liaison officer for all queries and requests coming from the eastern and northern fronts. General Pretender then informed the freedom fighters at their headquarters that he was now in charge, using the fewest words possible. He told the switchboard, 'The head of police is fatigued, so please do not disturb him unnecessarily,' and then he contacted other police and army headquarters in the country to order that all arms, ammunition, grenades and mines locked up in the arsenals because of the rash of robberies of military equipment all over the country.

He further explained that positions and movements of freedom fighters were not clearly known at this time, except where there had been ambushes and road incidents. Likewise, army units were told to carry ammunition only for patrol duty, absolutely and unconditionally; no extra supplies were to be carried in lorries, infantry carriers or tanks. The next important step was to inform military headquarters that intelligence indicated a massive secondary invasion building up on the north-eastern border area and the south-eastern area next to Swaziland. All available military were to be diverted to these areas immediately. The orders were dutifully carried out in response the stern and authoritative voice of the new pretender.

At five o'clock, the new general informed the second in command that he wanted only a skeleton staff to remain: all personnel were to proceed to town police stations away from the centre and to roadblocks at staggered hours before coming to HQ for further orders. Only eight policemen were left at HQ. Cronje and 'van Wyk' had no trouble in packing the now retired commandant's body into a golf bag brought up by Tommy Mthethwa, removing any additional blood spots and returning to their BMW in the basement underground quite undetected.

Mrs Wilkinson had rung up at 3 p.m. to ask how the general was managing and was told rather gruffly that he was busy, 'darling', and that he would not be able to visit tonight nor the next night. She was to please be patient, 'darling', because he would come to visit her 'some time' as soon as he was free. George Olivier was able to copy her lover's voice pretty well. It was easier on the telephone than speaking face to face, but Mrs Wilkinson was not quite convinced and wondered if he was assuming a new pose or a new role after their passionate dalliance of six months. She wondered if it might be the widow Renée, that scheming little bitch who only just recently lost her husband on the eastern border within a few days of the start of operations. Might she have been able to win his affections as quickly as she had with Captain Van Niekerk soon after her first widowhood following a car accident with husband number one?

She felt it was better to wait a day or two before barging into police headquarters with a demand to see her dear, good friend who had come to mean so much to her. It was a fact that the voice of her dear friend did lack the affection and authority to which she had become accustomed in the last few months.

Ah well, she thought, I'll just have to be brave and patient.

Already her children were getting used to seeing General J van Wyk at their house and home without showing any resentment; it was not as if he were intruding. It would be most unfortunate if this great friendship should go awry, she thought to herself, and then she might have to go through another kind of grief, keeping it to herself, without the companionship of friends to help her because it had been a somewhat irregular affair. It was most disheartening for Marie when she thought of all that might be going wrong; so it took all her will power to try to remain calm without throwing a sort of tantrum, and expressing fury at the cruel fate and misfortune that destiny seemed to be casting upon her.

Hit and Run

The eastern and northern campaigns were petering out. Pockets of resistance remained; the platoons of Major Labuschagne had been reinforced after a five-day delay. Helicopters had been largely successful in chasing freedom fighters into the hills, culverts and caves in spite of several losses. The wounded had been evacuated to military hospitals, most of them with feet blown off; the dead were to be buried with full military honours as soon as possible. One party that still eluded the South African army was a stick of men led by Pedro the leather man, much reduced after this first week of conflict. He had been a leather- and shoemaker during Portuguese colonial rule and carried with him an ardent hatred of all things colonial, whether Portuguese, British or Dutch. He did not care to distinguish between white groups. As he saw it, they were all shits, scum, interlopers, usurpers, adventurers or just contemptible.

Pedro always remembered during his leather-working days how farmers and wives of farmers or company bosses would order him to repair children's shoes right away. He had to stop everything else he was working on, as if they were the king of Monomatapa and then they would leave without paying; half an hour's work, then, 'Okay, Pedro, pay you some time later.' Some time later never came, while the poor of the district would always pay for their repairs, even if it meant going without food for an evening. But these white autocrats – he came to hate them. If they'd been polite, it might have been different, but most of them had no idea what politeness was; though, to be fair, he'd admit the widows and missionaries behaved well, but they were very much in the minority.

This same Pedro was delighted and ecstatic to be on the war-path after ten years with an auxiliary Frelimo military unit. He had had a stick of ten men with him when he had left, riding in a converted Chevrolet. They had captured the first border police post quite easily, had mined and booby-trapped it, then motored for about fifty kilometres until the radiator boiled over because of some bullet holes caused during a brief encounter with isolated gunmen they had hardly taken notice of since the shooting had been so sporadic. Soon after this, the engine had seized up, forcing his group to walk into the bushy forest keeping close to riverbeds, never to be far from water.

'Food you can do without for several days,' he used to say, 'but without water and walking in the sun's heat, after two days you are desperate; after three days you go crazy.'

So Pedro went on forwards still with his decimated stick of five men. Some had got separated by wandering apart; some were shot up by armed helicopter attacks. Pedro meant to stay and kill. He had notched up ten white soldiers killed, not nearly enough to avenge his anger against colonial rule. But he got no further. One bullet had grazed his temple, knocked him out and he was captured and his hands and feet tied up. He was stripped, questioned, bashed up bodily with rifle butts, but never had his head with his head wound struck. His head had to be left clear; his mind must be preserved. He pretended ignorance and non-understanding. 'Non comprehendo,' he answered to those speaking to him in Portuguese or Shangaan or Zulu. 'Non comprehendo, angasi luthu; nada a decir.'

They got nothing out of him except his wallet, penknife, socks and shoes. At 2 a.m., he wriggled and crawled out from under the canvas, freed his arms and legs very easily and slipped past the sleeping sentry and back to the trail. No contacts were possible now because he was unarmed and defenceless. He could just follow a stream, downstream this time, past the police frontier blockhouse now re-occupied and ready for action. So, he thought to himself, we've lost, it would seem.

Finally he got across the border to the local HQ in Mozambique, to be shouted at and berated by his CO who yelled at him for being obtuse, stubborn, self-willed and vindictive.

'You know,' shouted Colonel Wandile Dlamini. 'You know you were supposed to hit and run, hit and run until you were out of ammo, then come back to base. You went on hitting and advancing for two weeks. You were supposed to run back here to base here, instead of going on for one hundred and sixty kilometres. Now where is your stick of men? You have led them to be captured, wounded or killed. Only one has returned with a wound in his hand after your second contact; he lost you when you ran off westwards into the setting sun. And the other nine men? All gone, finished and lost. After four weeks there's no hope of their return, and whose fault is that?'

In this way, the colonel went on shouting at Pedro the leather man, one time corporal in charge of ten men, a section of a platoon.

But there was nothing to be done. Pedro admitted he had been wrong. But only because he was weak after the ordeal of his capture, beating up and then the long return back to base with only river water and loquat or marula berries to sustain him. It hadn't been much for an athletic soldier like Pedro.

'But I got my revenge!' he was exultant. 'Ten men were killed and their ammo and guns taken from them. I might have gone on if I had not been knocked out by a graze shot to the temple. Admittedly, I was either lucky not to be killed, or unlucky to be hit at all. That helped my revenge and anger enormously,' he replied.

Meanwhile, back in the South African camp from where he had escaped, Colonel Billingham was going through his possessions: socks, shoes, a handkerchief and shirt; not really significant; then a wallet containing 200 escudos in paper money, a victory medal from 1992, two paper clips and a note with the words 'Bater e Correr' printed out neatly on a square piece of paper.

'What the hell does this mean?' wondered the colonel. 'Is this campaign only a side show? There is no mention or implication of invasion and occupation, no suggestion of meeting up with forces in our country, nor plans for a united confrontation in the interior? I think there is something going on that we do not understand. We can only wait, but it is my guess that the real trouble is behind us.'

It was then that the company received the order from headquarters from General 'van Wyk' that all military forces were to remain in the field to oppose expected renewed attacks and opposition from the east and north.

The colonel believed there had been some almighty mess up, 'And we will have to pay the consequences, I'm telling you!'

But there was nothing else to do.

'Ours is not to question why, but to simply do or die,' or more appropriately, 'They also serve who stand and wait.' He muttered the quotes as some kind of reassurance to himself.

Impostor

George Olivier, alias General van Wyk, was able to return to HQ for three more days. He was able to parry questions on the phone in his assumed voice. All those who called into his office saw him with a handkerchief at his nose and received curt orders.

'I've told you what to do; all soldiers to the specified fronts; police at roadblocks and their stations; reinforcements when in dire need at weak points. Confer with Lieutenant Cronje on the second floor for details and explanations.'

Then, on his fourth day in power, Olivier got an urgent message brought to him by a courier running up ten floors, plus a phone call, in case the runner should fail. The message simply said, 'The duchess is coming.' He had time to don his overcoat, in spite of the hot weather, inform the security guards on the landing of his intended trip to the military section of the northern suburbs, and take the emergency stairway two steps at a time to avoid any possible encounter with the unknown lover of the now deceased general. It was a near thing.

To be discovered by Mrs Wilkinson, née Marais, or by Mrs van Wyk would have exposed all the plans of the freedom fighters with their concomitant misdirections issued from the top echelon. As he passed the second floor, he could hear the loud shrieks of an angry woman demanding to know if her dear good friend and compatriot was still well and healthy, as he had been four days ago. He passed the two windows letting on to the area with cap under his arm, looking away with a large hanky over his nose and mouth. It worked. He was not recognised and so reached the basement and was into the BMW, and out before any alarm was set off. In fact, the alarm was not given for another three days while the general's dear lover was eating her heart out, asking why there had been this complete change from closeness and intimacy to complete absence.

Three days later, even the police personnel were asking about the sudden absence of their general. They presumed he'd had a serious throat and head inflammation, hence the persistent handkerchief. So the authorities rang up his wife. She knew nothing about the general, had in fact lost interest in her husband for several months except to receive his salary into their joint account and anything else he might care to get her, which was very little now in the way of presents or thank you gifts. However, she started worrying that some disaster had come to him after these four days of total absence with no one able to inform her of his whereabouts so as to put her mind at rest. This had to be something different and serious. Although no longer a companion, he was still important to her as an influence on the children.

Of course, the general's body was never found. It had been buried at dead of night in his vest and pants far away, with guards up to two hundred metres away all around to prevent the possibility of other witnesses. Captain du Toit's disappearance also puzzled the colonels in charge. It was soon known that a Captain du Toit had been killed at a border post on the eastern front, with the same initials and same ID number as recorded at the police post and the HQ office. So this man had been an impostor, that was finally and certainly agreed upon. So if Captain du Toit was an impostor, could the lieutenant also have been an impostor? It was curious what a close liaison there had been between the general and the lieutenant during the four days of their presence.

All personnel in the army and police were checked to see who might have been impersonating the disappeared lieutenant and no one was found to have been absent for four days.

The incident remained a mystery until forty years later when a friend's father, a one-time freedom fighter, admitted to friends and their children that the said chief had been killed, spirited away and impersonated for four days by an amateur actor and ex-army chancer from Cape Town. It was a cause of laughter for many, but, for the police, then and later, it became an acute embarrassment which was hushed up and never disclosed to any public press conference nor at any meetings, in order to avoid loss of confidence in the combined police and armed forces of the country. Of course, security was tightened all over the services, with checks on who was impersonating whom, with demands for the production of ID papers on the spot. Many were found suspect, but never confirmed as spies or impostors; the papers were defective or not up to date or belonged to another soldier of the same rank. It was an example of closing the stable door after the horse had bolted.

Camp Invasions

Meanwhile, as many army units went on wild goose chases in the northern, southern and eastern areas, and found only peace and quiet, with no disturbances and certainly no invading army, the forces of the Polygonian Freedom Fighters moved en masse into army barracks to clear out skeleton forces, and take over and occupy many police stations all over the country; which stations had also been reduced to a skeleton staff. They were able to open dozens of arsenals, empty out the contents and stand armed to the teeth while the other army units were spending their ammunition into the air in the countryside as a form of recreation, since there was nothing else to do. Later, after thorough reconnaissance into the area where they had been ordered to go, and with no further directives coming from headquarters under the command of General 'van Wyk', they returned to base to find their entry blocked by black soldiers wearing a sort of dark blue military gear. They were denied entry into the military bases, and threatened with close or mid-distance gunfire if they should try to get close or indulge in any military manoeuvre. They camped where they were safe and waited, the only action worth calling a strategy, and they were rewarded.

Although the blacks looked menacing and united, they were far and away from being that. The Zulus demanded command and control; the Xhosas wanted their country, Transkei, as a self-ruling state as it had been for fifteen years; the Sothos insisted on keeping Northern Polygonia as their own country; and the Tswanas were returning home into their western provinces because they were not receiving their portions of food, equipment and pay.

That was when the SADOFAC burst into action. Hearing that their country's military bases had been taken by black troops who gave no quarter and were demanding a truce around a conference table, they assembled and organised themselves in the matter of half a day. With their less modern weapons, for they had mostly hunting guns and revolvers carried for personal protection, they were able to assemble in over half the army camps, to penetrate under fences or over brick walls and across roofs where they were least expected during the night and morning after the alarm had been given. The blacks tried to retaliate with small-arms fire and the use of Ferrets, with their rubber wheels, single driver, and a gunner in front manning a Browning .50 machine gun. This was no deterrent to young men fighting for their country. The young men simply climbed on top of the Ferrets from behind, smeared the front windows with mud and clay, broke off the windscreen wipers at the same time, and the Ferrets then became useless. Neither driver nor gunner could see ahead, so that the machine guns were fired wildly and were easily avoided. The pair inside simply had to surrender by opening up the trapdoor and pushing up a white cloth tied on the longest spanner they could find.

Marius Wessels, who thought he knew most of the influences operating in his country, was most surprised to see this spontaneous leap to arms all over the country. He studied all information coming through army intelligence headquarters and admitted that what he had suspected was only a quarter of what had actually developed.

There were casualties on both sides; treated at the nearest hospitals no matter what their ethnic groups. Prisoners were taken and mixed up with criminals. Black prisoners found themselves sharing with white soldiers of the old army who had been captured after ambushes, sometimes with very little fighting, because of ammunition shortage. Black casualties were hurriedly put into army wards to find whites had been put there before them and left unattended until their colleagues in arms sorted out who belonged where. There was an almighty mix-up with different groups claiming authority and command when in fact they were quite incapable of exercising it.

In the general mêlée, some camps were soon back in the hands and under the command of the regular units together with the army units of SADOFAC youngsters. Other camps remained under the control of the black amateur-turned-professional soldiers. They were able to keep command because they were far from towns and villagers from which counter-action might have captured them. Such camps were near desert areas, singled out originally for their isolated positions as a means of secrecy. Such was the national mix-up, with the military following common sense as far as it was possible. Since the politicians had gone into a phase of non-interference, waiting to see what would happen, so had the leading military commanders. It was like a war game, moving pieces with no one getting killed any more.

Many were wondering what was going on, since accurate information was unobtainable, or was being suppressed by the official news censors. So the often repeated questions were, 'How will all this finish?' or 'What is going to happen next?'

It was not long before these questions were answered.

'Patience also rewards the brave!'

Turmoil

In this state of military turmoil, the ordinary life of the country continued much as before, with public and private services very much the same, although there was a constant atmosphere of impending disaster. Trading, school and university education, agriculture and medical services went on as before, as if little had happened. The police force had returned to its usual activities of stopping or catching criminals, traffic control and checking illicit drug imports. The police force had come to realise it was no longer necessary to chase after spurious invasions from the east nor to involve itself with military concerns all over the country, since the national army was quite capable of doing this, as it was their main responsibility.

But everyone, that is, all the reading public, plus many more like television watchers and wireless listeners, were all well aware that there was a national civil war among the various and differing military attachments.

In Camp Warsaw, near Johannesburg, so called because many Polish immigrants had helped to build the army camp after World War Two for the housing and training of troops to protect the large gold mining complexes not so far away, there occurred results rather typical of new developments then taking place.

The camp, occupied by the Polygonian Freedom Fighters, had been invaded during the night by the young people of SADOFAC, who had cleared the main area of their enemies. Resistance persisted among buildings and trenches around the periphery. The real national army had driven in and taken over from the amateur forces to try to overcome any resistance still remaining. Groups of black soldiers in dark blue uniforms were surrendering when their position was obviously hopeless. Their local leaders encouraged them to stop the killing of themselves and others. 'Better to give up now when we can't win, so that we might live to fight to our advantage another time.' The army commanders were glad to receive these men, to disarm them and get them locked up in the local army prison.

Here Major Marius Wessels, for that was his military rank when seconded to army manoeuvres, was most interested to notice all that was going on. As one group approached, Jack Lessing, a coloured man with the intelligence department of the army walking alongside Marius, grabbed his elbow and spoke to him softly, but with some urgency. Jack was very much on the side of the national army against the freedom fighters. This was because of the dreadful killings his family had suffered in the past north of Cape Town, where Xhosa Africans had claimed land and stolen cattle and sheep belonging to his own people over the past century and more. They had stolen and killed farm stock from land which before had been scrub, sand dunes, hillocks and forest lands, occupied by straying nomadic bands living on what they could kill or capture. These lands stretched hundreds of kilometres north and east from where the Lessing family had settled over a century ago before.

Jack Lessing was one of many people who were the result of the early matings of Dutch, French or English sailors at the Cape after their sex-starved journeys from Europe southwards or from the East Indies travelling westwards. These hardy sailors found the black natives attractive with their early bosom development and their broad bums and natural charm typical of those who lived close to nature. They carried a perfume similar to the sweaty winners one can perceive after an Epsom Derby or at the races at Longchamp. Their offspring were accepted variously by the black peoples or the settled immigrants. They were called coloureds in South Africa, and over time they developed their own society.

Jack Lessing, as a result of his own varied experiences, was fluent in Dutch-Afrikaans and quite at home in English and the Xhosa language, an extremely useful asset when these three languages were so much in current use throughout the country. He also understood Zulu because Zulu and Xhosa speech are really similar. Hence, Jack was a most valuable asset to the intelligence branch of the army and not only because of his language abilities, but also because of his sincere allegiance to the ruling establishment, mixed with a deep distrust of these blacks whom he considered more of a menace than as soul brothers and sisters. It was not that he hated them. No! It was not a case of hating these numerous blacks and their many different tribes and subtribes throughout the country. It was simply a question of not trusting them unless one got to known them personally over time, and that meant them knowing him and his group; then and only then would there be trust.

Confrontation

Jack Lessing spoke to Marius Wessels earnestly while holding him briefly by his left elbow to draw his attention.

'Do you see that black man coming towards us about fifty metres away with a group of men on either side of him? The one with the red star in the centre of his beret. I know about him. He's the one they call the "Chimney Conductor", alias Joseph Khuzwayo. Do you remember him? He is from Natal, from a little place called Esigodeni, about three hundred and fifty kilometres from here in a south-easterly direction. Your men questioned him about three years ago with a two-day dry-out and intensive grilling, without getting any information out of him. I have been to visit his small shop since then, dressed up as a worker as if I were from the local quarry-cement factory nearby. He was quite in command of his trade and of his business, but more striking was the real respect and esteem everyone held him in without any sense of cowering, fawning or grovelling adulation. He was esteemed because he was a true leader. See what a position of command he has now.'

In fact, Joseph was now a commandant, equivalent to a major in the US army, with five hundred men under his command until they were cornered in the trenches at Camp Warsaw.

'Some people say he procured a *sangoma*, that is, a witch doctor, to create confusion in the mind of our late general J van Wyk during his last days in power at police headquarters.' Jack continued talking all the time to Marius as the group in question were approaching slowly. 'I believe it was something much more devious than that, as if somebody else had stepped in without being detected, until his wife or woman friend moved in to investigate, and then this somebody disappeared for ever, and General van Wyk has never been seen or heard of since. Have you heard about this strange influence at headquarters?' asked Jack, and the major nodded in the affirmative.

With this revelation, Marius Wessels flew into a rage when he realised how much had escaped his attention and his influence. He picked up an iron rod lying nearby, a small crowbar used for shifting weights about, and with a swing worthy of a backhand stroke in tennis, at which he had excelled during his postgraduate days at Cambridge, he delivered a powerful backhand swing into Joseph's right arm, who was quite near now, causing a deep gash into the skin and muscle of the right upper arm, rendering the arm useless while blood poured out of the wound.

Shouting with pain, but still brave and courageous as his father had taught him to be, Joseph smashed his left fist into Marius's right ear, causing an immediate rupture of the eardrum followed by a copious haemorrhage through the external canal, which had Marius yelling with pain as his hand closed over his ear in an act of protection that came too late.

That's when Marius starting abusing his adversaries, cursing the revolutionaries and accusing them of being interested only in promoting their own cause while content to destroy the country where they had been protected and had prospered. Joseph likewise delivered a barrage of abuse, saying how his people had suffered loss of freedom for long enough, being fenced off from large areas or cramped into small places when there were huge places for everyone else, and had further been refused correct representation in public affairs and had the opinions of his own people, as well as those of thousands of others, utterly ignored.

While this slanging match was going on with the two antagonists in great pain and in a great state of anger, all the other soldiers on both sides stood silently by, hoping this was not another start to military involvement, but waiting to see what would develop. It was then that Colonel Billingham, in charge of the camp, came out of the offices close by to check the fracas that was audible all around the camp. He ordered loudly that it was the decision of the then president, supported by general agreement at a recent parliamentary meeting, that all conflict was to be stopped and a conference arranged at each and every place where there was military confrontation. He told the two men to report to the medical centres, Joseph at the camp's medical centre, Marius at the regimental first-aid post, quite nearby.

Unification

So it was that Peter Kruger, the great-grandson of the famous Paul Kruger, spoke at Camp Warsaw the following morning, and his speech was relayed simultaneously over the radio and on television at nine o'clock. It suggested a rapprochement, with conferences at all important municipal areas throughout the country among all the different groups who had been involved in military combat during the last three weeks.

Paul Kruger had been a great leader during the last century in the northern provinces, helping to organise the railways being built by mining companies all over the country to form an efficient network and transport system from mines to towns to harbours. Likewise, Paul had been successful in encouraging farming: cattle breeding, sheep, cotton, tobacco, winter wheat and that favourite food of all blacks, the maize plant to provide the stodgy porridge *putu*, a staple diet for them. Paul ended his career as political leader against the invading British who had taken over his country after three years of lethal fighting and indulged in a form of genocide before anyone else had thought of trying this. He had had to leave, a broken man, retreating through Mozambique to Switzerland, to end his days among the Calvinists of Geneva.

Kruger's great-grandson was of a similar mould, though adapted to the present time. His speech exhorted communication, trust and cooperation. He stated how the efforts of the freedom fighters had shown them to be capable of mass action with significant success. He held his countrymen in respect and he was in favour of worthwhile agreements among all its people. He said clearly that further conflict was of no use or gain to anyone, and that it was necessary to abolish the rigid system of separate development which had now come to be so hateful and hurtful to peace-loving and respectable citizens. He declared that each and every person must be considered as deserving dignity and respect.

It would be necessary to cooperate and readjust so that there were no longer separate beaches, buses, schools, hospitals, pubs and hotels, and so on. All must now be integrated. But this required respect from everyone towards everyone. Horseplay could be tolerated only so long as it remained a form of entertainment. However, misbehaviour, hooliganism and vandalism would not be tolerated.

Toilets would likewise be integrated but must be used in the proper way. If toilet attendants couldn't direct users towards correct usage, if there were messes on the lavatory floors and on tops of lids instead of underneath, there would have to be created separate black lavatories appropriate for the squatting crapping position instead of the more usual sitting pose.

Thus he went on talking. Another subject he touched on was that of language, as follows. 'Likewise, there will be endless arguments about the primacy of one language. I say it is normal that each group will value its own language above all others. But with eleven different languages, no one of them will become a primary one except in private homes and small schools. In law courts, special allowance will be given to those who only speak one language, otherwise it will be Afrikaans or English that is to be in general use. Think, all you people. If anyone should wish to continue education, and I hope all will be continuing until the age of sixteen, and many further into university studies; all these studies are in English or Afrikaans. There are no textbooks for the study of geography or history, economics, physics or chemistry in any language other than English or Afrikaans, and even the latter is losing some of its ascendancy.

'We will develop cooperation with a national voting system, I say in two or three years' time when parties and candidates will have been arranged, established and finally voted for in a democratic system. We have learned what it means to be in conflict. Many have lost their lives during the last month, some have even disappeared, perhaps never to be seen again. We must accept this as a form of suffering and grief to encourage us to work so that we can be reconciled in the future. What good is fighting if nobody wins?'

Land reform was the biggest project for the new government,

especially how to redistribute land to many hundreds, perhaps thousands, who would want to make claims of ownership to land that belonged to their fathers or forefathers. So much land had been taken over by scientific farmers producing milk, maize, beef cattle or sugar to supply the country's needs. Were these lands to be handed back to subsistence farmers who would only produce enough for their own family and local clan? Mr Peter Kruger said the question of land ownership would be considered seriously and compromise reached to satisfy as many as possible.

As for sport, that was a much easier subject to broach with regard to integration. All sports clubs would admit whoever asked in keeping with the club regulations, regardless of race, colour, creed and sex. Selection of provincial and national teams would be quite simply based on merit. 'May the best player win!' Mr Kruger expected the Olympic Games to be opened to our country again, as they had been twenty-five years before. 'Then we will be glad to see how our athletes compare with those of other countries!'

By now it was the time for black leaders to welcome a new eager and integrated Polygonia. As it was, after three weeks of internal strife including an eastern invasion, before which there had been tight security throughout the country with regards to segregation and separation, it was to be expected that the real black leaders were not available for public speaking. They had yet to be brought forward, primed and offered leadership. So it was that the local leaders were asked to give a speech of sorts, improvised and really spontaneous for the occasion. It happened that Joseph Khuzwayo was selected to speak since he was the best educated in his group, albeit mostly self-educated but capable anyway, and much better equipped to talk than anyone else in his group around Camp Warsaw and beyond.

'Good comrades, brothers and sisters, compatriots in arms, countrymen, friends, all of good intentions,' started Joseph, with his right arm in bandages. 'It gives me tremendous pleasure and pride to see how well you have managed to conduct yourselves in a true military manner and with some military success. Now we can start to be as one country, to feel as one country, with each affording respect and decency to everyone else. From what Mr

Kruger tells us, we will be able to cooperate with dialogue. At conference tables, we will be treated as responsible citizens. Thanks to our brave efforts, we have been able to create an influence suitable to convince hundreds that we do not have to go on living separately in a fragmented horrible arrangement called apartheid. We can be all together now without rancour or jealousy. We must continue in a way that is suitable and acceptable. We do not want to antagonise further. We can be ourselves now, all of us, as true Polygonians.'

Joseph's speech was greeted with screams of delight and shouts of, 'Bravo! Well done, Joe. Hurrah for the "Chimney Conductor". Viva for Joseph! Viva Polygonia! Long live Polygonia!'

It was then that the regimental band struck up tunes to reinforce the goodwill of all present and swell the hearts of so many with gladness for the promised general peace and unification. The first tune was the one so beloved of all African freedom fighters:

> Nkosi sikele l'i Africa,
> Malupaka nyiswu dumo lwayo;
> Yizwa imithanda zoyetu,
> Nkosi sikelela, Nkosi sikelela.

A free translation goes:

> God bless Africa,
> Let her fame spread far and wide;
> Hear our prayer,
> May God bless us.
> Come, spirit, come, come, Holy Spirit,
> Come and bless us, our children.

To go with this fine song an English one was found for the occasion. The song of the British Grenadiers was chosen as suitable, with an ending to correspond to the present event.

> Some speak of Alexander and some of Hercules,
> Of Hector and Lysander and such great men as these.
> But of the world's great heroes,
> There's none that can compare,

With the Poly, Poly, Poly, Poly, Polygonians.

Amid huge cheers, cap throwing, and more shouts of 'Viva Africa, Viva Polygonia,' the crowds were dispersed with the leaders each going their own appointed ways followed by their own men, each man glad and hopeful for the unification and cooperation as promised for everyone's future.

Bibliography

Carew Hunt, R.N., *The Theory and Practice of Communism*, Harmondsworth, Penguin, 1963

Daniel-Rops, H., *The Church in a Age of Revolution – 1789–1870*, Letchworth, J.M. Dent & Sons, 1965

Raven-Hart, Major R., *Before van Riebeeck*, Cape Town, C Struick, 1967

Razinsky, Edvard, *Stalin*, London, Hodder & Stoughton, 1997

Remnick, David, *Lenin's Tomb*, London, Penguin, 1994